Penguin Books
The End of a Mission

Heinrich Böll was born in Cologne in 1917. The son of
a sculptor, he began work in a bookshop, then served
in the infantry throughout the war. After 1945 he took
various jobs, becoming a freelance writer in 1951. He
has since worked as a novelist, short-story writer and radio
playwright. His first novels, *The Train Was on Time*
and *And Where Were You, Adam?* concerned the despair
of those involved in total war; his later works, including
Acquainted with the Night and *The Unguarded House*,
deal with the moral vacuum behind the post-war
'economic miracle' in Western Germany. In his short-story
writing Böll is regarded as one of the founders of the
contemporary German American-style '*Kurzgeschichte*'.
Among his other novels are *Group Portrait with Lady*
(1973), *Children are Civilians Too* (1973) and *The Lost
Honour of Katharina Blum* (1974). Heinrich Böll was
elected the first Neil Gunn Fellow by the Scottish Arts
Council in 1970 and was awarded the Nobel Prize for
Literature in 1972.

Heinrich Böll

The End of a Mission

Translated from the German
by Leila Vennewitz

Penguin Books

Ende einer Dienstfahrt first published by
Kiepenheuer & Witsch, Köln-Berlin 1966

Penguin Books Ltd, Harmondsworth,
Middlesex, England
Penguin Books, 625 Madison Avenue,
New York, New York 10022, U.S.A.
Penguin Books Australia Ltd, Ringwood,
Victoria, Australia
Penguin Books Canada Ltd, 2801 John Street,
Markham, Ontario, Canada L3R 1B4
Penguin Books (N.Z.) Ltd, 182–190 Wairau Road,
Auckland 10, New Zealand

Translation published in Great Britain by
Weidenfeld & Nicolson 1968
Published in Penguin Books 1973
Reprinted 1974, 1977, 1978

Made and printed in Great Britain
by Richard Clay (The Chaucer Press) Ltd,
Bungay, Suffolk
Set in Linotype Plantin

Translator's Acknowledgement

I wish to express my deep gratitude
for all the help given me in this translation
by my husband, William Vennewitz.

                              Leila Vennewitz
Vancouver, Canada

List of Characters

The accused

Johann Gruhl, a cabinet-maker from the village of Huskirchen.
Georg Gruhl, his son, also a cabinet-maker; until recently a
    private first class in the German Army.

Persons associated with the County Court of Birglar

Dr Alois Stollfuss, the judge.
Dr Kugl-Egger, district attorney.
Dr Hermes, defence attorney.
Councillor Bergnolte, an observer from the city.
Herr Sterck, a sheriff's officer from the city.
Herr Schroer, the local sheriff's officer and warder of Birglar
    County jail.
Herr Aussem, court recorder and a junior barrister.

Witnesses

Herr Heuser, County Traffic Inspector.
Inspector Heinrich Kirffel, a police officer.
Herr Albert Erbel, a travelling salesman.
Detective Commissioner Schmulck.
Herr Hubert Hall, the bailiff.

Character witnesses

Frau Sanni Seiffert, owner of the Red Lantern.
Herr Erwin Horn, master of the Birglar carpenters' guild.
Private First Class Kuttke.
Sergeant Behlau.
First Lieutenant Heimüller, Gruhl junior's superior officer.
Father Kolb, the Huskirchen parish priest.

Expert witnesses

Dr Grähn, an economist and auditor.
Herr Kirffel, an income tax inspector; son of Inspector Kirffel.
Professor Büren, an art professor.

Others

Herr Herbert Hollweg, editor of the *Duhr Valley Courier*.
Herr Wolfgang Brehsel, a reporter.
Frau Marlies Hermes, the defence attorney's wife.
Frau Else Kugl-Egger, the district attorney's wife.
Fräulein Agnes Hall, the judge's cousin.
Herr Grellber, a political figure in the city.
Herr and Frau Schmitz, proprietors of the Duhr Terraces
    restaurant in Birglar.
Eva Schmitz, their daughter.
Frau Wermelskirchen, Gruhl senior's neighbour.
Frau Leuffen, Gruhl senior's mother-in-law.
Frau Schorf-Kreidel, wife of the driver of the Mercedes 300.
Herr and Frau Frohn, owners of Frohn's Bakery.
Frau Grete Horn, wife of the master of the carpenters' guild.
Frau Kirffel, the income tax inspector's wife.
Frau Lisa Schroer, the sheriff's officer's wife.
Frau Maria Stollfuss, the judge's wife.
Huppenach, a young farmer.
Herr Motrik, an art dealer.
Frau Hall, the bailiff's wife.

One

In the early fall of last year a trial took place at the County Court of Birglar about which the public heard very little. The three newspapers circulating in Birglar County, the *Rhineland Review*, the *Rhineland Daily News*, and the *Duhr Valley Courier*, sometimes published lengthy reports on cattle thefts, major traffic offences, and county fair brawls in their columns 'From the Courtroom', 'In the Courtroom', and 'Courtroom News', but in this instance they printed only a brief account which, strangely enough, was identical in all three papers:

Johann and Georg Gruhl, father and son, appeared before a lenient judge. One of the favourite personalities in the public life of our town, County Court Judge Dr Stollfuss (who will be duly honoured in a subsequent issue) conducted the trial of Johann and Georg Gruhl of Huskirchen, whose inexplicable behaviour last June gave rise to considerable alarm in some quarters. The trial, Judge Stollfuss's final one before his retirement, lasted one day, and the two Gruhls were sentenced to full restitution of property and six weeks' imprisonment. After conferring briefly with their defence attorney, Dr Hermes of Birglar, the two men accepted the light sentence. With the period of remand custody being taken into account, they could be released immediately.

The local editors of the *Rhineland Review* and the *Rhineland Daily News* had already agreed some weeks before the trial began that they would not compete in this matter, that they would not 'play up' the Gruhl case, there 'wasn't enough in it'. If – which was not likely to happen – readers complained about the absence of reports on the Gruhl trial, both editors were ready with an excuse which, as Krichel, the *Review* editor, said, 'fitted as snugly as the boots of a champion skater': the trial of Schewen, the child murderer, in the neighbouring city was due to open at the same time and would interest a wider circle of readers. The two editors failed to arrive at a similar arrangement with Dr Hollweg, editor in chief, publisher, and printer of the *Duhr Valley Courier*. Dr Hollweg, who carried on a kind of Liberal opposition in Birglar County, suspected – not without reason – a 'clerical-socialist' conspiracy, and told Wolfgang Brehsel, his current reporter and a former student of Protestant theology, to plan to cover the trial. Brehsel, who preferred court reporting to all other kinds, found out the date of the trial – set earlier than expected – from Frau Hermes, the defence attorney's wife; furthermore, after attending a lecture on 'The Church Council and Non-Christians', and while sitting over a glass of beer with the speaker, a prelate by the name of Dr Kerb, she had explained the really interesting aspects of the Gruhl case to Brehsel: the full confession of the accused, their offence, their personalities, but above all the fact that the prosecution wished to see the strange action of the Gruhls condemned merely as 'property damage and public mischief', while ignoring the obvious fact of arson. Moreover, Frau Hermes, herself an honours graduate in law, also found it strange that the trial date should have been set so quickly, and that the accused should be housed in one of the few cells in the courthouse where, as all Birglar knew, they were living off the fat of the land; and Frau Hermes found it particularly strange that this trial should take place in a county court before Judge Stollfuss, who was on the point of retirement and was both noted and notorious for his humanitarian dealings past and present. Even Brehsel, although he was just starting to find his way in the legal world, felt that a crime of this kind warranted at least a jury as against a single judge; Frau Hermes confirmed this, turned to the speaker of the evening, Dr Kerb, who was beginning to feel bored by this local Birglar gossip, and asked him to give the non-Catholic but ecumenically interested Brehsel a few pointers for his article on the lecture.

That same evening Brehsel had gone to the office and discussed the finer legal points of the Gruhl case with his boss, Dr Hollweg. At the same time Hollweg, who liked to show that he had learned the trades of printing and typesetting 'from the ground up', sat at the Linotype machine composing the article on the evening's lecture at Brehsel's dictation. Hollweg, to whom Brehsel's enthusiasm appealed, although it sometimes 'got on his nerves', as he said, altered the phrase 'very optimistic' to 'with a certain degree of hopefulness', and 'magnificent liberality' to 'with a certain candour', and instructed Brehsel to cover the Gruhl trial for the *Duhr Valley Courier*. Then he washed his hands with that childlike pleasure that overcame him whenever he had soiled his hands by genuine down-to-earth work, got into his car, and drove the few miles to Kireskirchen to the home of his friend, a member of the legislature and a Liberal like himself, who had invited him to dinner.

Hollweg, a jovial, affable, though somewhat indolent man in his early fifties, had no idea that he was saving his friend considerable anxiety by being the first to bring up the subject of the strange case of the Gruhls. He expressed his astonishment at the leniency of the state – whose severity he invariably exposed whenever it was manifested and which one really had to keep an eye on – in this case; he found this accommodating attitude on the part of the state as suspect as excessive severity; and as a Liberal he felt constrained to lay his finger on this wound too. Hollweg, who was inclined to become garrulous, was advised by his friend in his customary courteous manner not to overestimate events in Birglar County, as sometimes happened to him – for example, in the case of Heinrich Grabel of Dulbenweiler, in whom he had immediately seen a martyr to the cause of liberty but who turned out to be a petty swindler, a self-important little man with 'rather an open hand for money from the wrong quarter'. Hollweg did not like to be reminded of Heinrich Grabel; he had gone all out for him, given him publicity, recommended him to colleagues on other newspapers, even persuaded the correspondent for a national daily to take an interest in him. He kissed the hand of his hostess, who was yawning and begged to be excused – she had been up all night at their little girl's bedside – and turned his attention for a time to the cheese, a Camembert garnished with paprika and onions and accompanied by a glass of good red wine. His friend refilled his glass, saying: 'If I were you, I'd stay clear of those Gruhls.' But Hollweg replied that a challenge of that kind, behind which – he wasn't that dumb – he suspected an ulterior motive, a warning of that kind was for him, passionate Liberal and journalist that he was, an incentive to take up the affair. His host became serious and said: 'Listen, Herbert, have I ever asked you a favour where your paper's concerned?' Hollweg, taken aback, said no, he never had. *Now*, said his host, he was asking him for something for the first time, 'and it's for your own sake'. Hollweg, who was often enough teased for his local patriotism and was sensitive about his provincial outlook, promised to call off his reporter, but on condition that his friend would explain what was behind it all. There was nothing behind it, he said; Hollweg could go there if he liked, listen to the proceedings, and judge for himself whether they were worth reporting; it was just that it was foolish for any reporter to blow up the affair. The mere thought of the courtroom made Hollweg yawn: that stuffy building next door to the church, still smelling of school; old Dr Stollfuss, his cousin Agnes Hall an inevitable spectator, and besides: wasn't it a good thing for the Gruhls to come before a lenient judge and be spared publicity? Furthermore, it would be a blessing for all lovers of antique furniture in Birglar County and beyond if Gruhl senior were free again – his skilful hands, his infallible taste, once more at the service of the community.

Over coffee, which the host poured from a Thermos jug in the study, he asked Hollweg whether he remembered a certain Betty Hall of Kireskirchen, who had later become an actress. No, said Hollweg, no doubt his friend was forgetting the difference in their ages, which was fifteen years after all; anyway, what about this Hall girl? She was appearing, his friend said, in the city in a Polish play and had had excellent reviews. Hollweg accepted the invitation to the theatre.

At seven-thirty next morning Brehsel received a phone call from Hollweg telling him not to cover the Gruhl case in Birglar but to go to the city instead, where the sensational trial of Schewen, the child murderer, was opening at the same hour. For a moment or two Brehsel wondered why his boss, who was known to be a late riser, should call him so early in the morning, until it occurred to him that late risers usually go to bed late, and it was possible that Hollweg had just got home. Hollweg's voice seemed to him a shade too forceful, almost peremptory, subtle differences that surprised him; Hollweg was usually an easy-going man, not very forceful, who only tended to get excited when three of four cancellations came in on the same day. Brehsel did not waste much time thinking about these minimal deviations from the norm; he shaved, had breakfast, and drove in his small car to the city; he felt some apprehension at the parking problem facing him, also because he was afraid of the reporters of international repute who had announced their arrival from all over the world. A press card was waiting for him, as Hollweg had assured him it would be; the member of the legislature, who was a member of the defence committee and the press committee, had made some phone calls early that morning and used his influence to obtain a card.

The Gruhl trial took place in the smallest of the three available rooms in the presence of ten spectators, almost all of whom were related to the accused, the witnesses, or other persons associated with the court or trial. Only one of those present was a stranger, a middle-aged man of light build, dressed in quiet good taste, whom only the judge, the district attorney, and the defence attorney knew to be Councillor Bergnolte from the neighbouring city.

The room in which the witnesses waited – the former teachers' common room of the school, which had been built for four classes in the eighties, expanded to take six classes at the turn of the century, and in the late fifties of this century replaced by a new building and handed over to the proverbially impoverished law court authorities, who had been carrying on

13

the administration of justice in a former school for non-commissioned officers – into this room, designed for six people or at most eight, were crowded fourteen persons of varying social and moral calibre: old Father Kolb of Huskirchen, two of his women parishioners, one of whom enjoyed the reputation of legendary respectability and piety, the other the reputation of being a super-sensual person, the term *super* implying a comparative of sensual rather than meta-sensual. The others consisted of: an officer, sergeant, and private first class of the German Army; an auditor, a bailiff, an income tax inspector, a travelling salesman, a county traffic inspector, the master of the carpenters' guild, a police inspector, and the proprietress of a bar.

When the trial opened, Sterck, the sheriff's officer, who had been brought over from the city especially for this purpose, had to forbid the witnesses from walking up and down the corridor; when voices were raised in the courtroom, proceedings became audible in the corridor. In the past this had led to some fruitless controversies between the judge and his superiors. Since in the cases of theft, inheritance disputes, and traffic offences the court's only chance of discovering the truth lay in bringing to light contradictory evidence, a sheriff's officer usually had to be asked to stand guard over the witnesses, and he often had to deal far more severely with the witnesses than his colleague inside the courtroom did with the accused. Sometimes there were fights in the witness room, heated abuse, invective, and insinuations. The sole advantage of the superannuated school building consisted in the fact – which was repeatedly stated in petitions – that there was 'no lack of toilets'. In the city, where the district court was housed in a new building that apparently did not have enough toilets, it was a standard joke to advise anyone who complained about this deficiency to take a taxi to Birglar, which was only fifteen miles away and where there was a notorious surplus of toilets at the exclusive disposal of the law.

The atmosphere among the spectators in the courtroom was reminiscent of an amateur dramatic company about to perform

14

a play from the classical repertory; a certain well-disposed excitement that derives its balance from the absence of risk in the enterprise: the audience knows the story, the roles and who is playing them, and that no surprises are in store. Yet still there is an air of expectancy; if it is a flop, not much has been lost, at most a little good-hearted enthusiasm; if it is a success, so much the better. By devious routes, the direct or indirect indiscretions that are inevitable in small communities had acquainted everyone present with the results of the preliminary inquiry. Everyone knew that both accused men had made a full confession; not only, as the district attorney had confided to a group of friends a few days previously, had they made 'a fuller confession' than any accused he had ever encountered: no, they had made 'by far the fullest confession'; during the preliminary inquiry they had contradicted neither the witnesses nor the experts. It would, the district attorney said, turn out to be one of those smooth, easy trials that arouse the suspicions of every experienced lawyer.

Of those present in the courtroom, only three were aware of what was undoubtedly known 'down there' – the customary expression for the neighbouring city – that, by charging the accused merely with property damage and public mischief and ignoring the aspect of arson, and by having only one judge conduct the trial, the state was playing a subtle game. The two people in a position to know something of the background were the district attorney's wife, Frau Kugl-Egger, who had moved to Birglar only a few days before, her husband having finally found an apartment, and the defence attorney's wife, Frau Hermes, the daughter of a Birglar businessman, who had already told all she knew to Brehsel the previous evening: that it had been decided 'down there' not to bring the case before either a jury or – what would have been quite 'appropriate' – a superior criminal court. But, she said, since it was known that no defence attorney was so perverse as to drag his clients before that 'miserable cur' Prell in the inferior criminal court when he had the chance of seeing them sentenced by a tired, kindly old lion like Stollfuss, it had been decided 'down there' to play the

Gruhl case down; this betokened a tacit but palpable concession and at the same time a request for concession; however, Hermes, her husband, reserved the right, depending on the outcome of the case, to reject both concession and request for concession, and to insist on a new trial, at the very least before a jury.

The third person among the spectators who was in the know, Councillor Bergnolte, would have been incapable of formulating such ideas; a man of great perceptive intelligence and a prodigious knowledge of the law, he naturally understood what was going on: that in this case justice, empowered to reinstate law and order, had, as a colleague had put it, come down 'off its high horse', although in this context he would have called such notions as concession, let alone request for concession, inadmissible.

When the judge and the district attorney entered and went to their seats and the spectators rose to their feet, the way in which they stood up and sat down again revealed that familiar indifference observed otherwise only in monasteries, where ritual has become a series of friendly gestures among intimates. Even when the accused were led in, there was no added stir; almost everyone there knew them and also knew that, during their ten weeks of remand custody, a young lady, one of the prettiest girls ever to have grown up in Birglar County, had brought them their breakfast, lunch, and dinner from the best restaurant in town. For twenty-two years, since the death of their wife and mother, they had not been as well looked after as they were during their confinement; it was even rumoured that occasionally, when there happened to be no other prisoners there whose discretion might have been suspect, they were allowed into the living room of Herr Schroer, the sheriff's officer, to watch some popular television programme. Schroer and his wife did in fact deny these rumours, but not very strenuously.

The only ones who did not know the accused were the district attorney's wife and Bergnolte; the district attorney's wife confessed to her husband at lunch that she had immediately felt greatly drawn to both the accused. That evening Bergnolte described his own impression as 'favourable, although against my inclination'. The two men appeared to be in good health; they were well-dressed, clean, and calm; they seemed not only composed but cheerful.

The process of identification was carried out with hardly a hitch; apart from the fact that Dr Stollfuss had to do what he usually had to do – request the accused to speak louder and more distinctly, and not to lapse too often into the thick regional dialect – and apart from the fact that from time to time dialect expressions had to be translated for the benefit of the district attorney, a stranger to the area, nothing very noteworthy occurred, nor was much new information produced. Gruhl senior, who gave his first names as *Johann* Heinrich Georg and his age as fifty, a slight, almost frail man of medium height whose bald head shimmered darkly, said before beginning his statement that he wanted to say something which he hoped His Honour, whom he knew and admired, indeed respected, would not hold against him; what he had to say was the truth, the whole truth, and nothing but the truth, although the information was very personal; but what he wanted to say was this: he didn't care two hoots for justice and the law, and even now he wouldn't be making a statement, or even giving his name, if – and these remarks, understood by hardly any of the spectators, were almost lost in Gruhl's soft, toneless delivery – if personal reasons were not involved. The first of these personal reasons was his great respect for His Honour; the second was his great respect for the witnesses, especially Inspector Kirffel, who had been a good, he might say a very good, friend of his father, a farmer from Dulbenweiler; nor did he want to let down or cause trouble to the other witnesses, Frau Leuffen, his mother-in-law, and Frau Wermelskirchen, his neighbour, and the witnesses Horn, Grähn, Hall, and Kirffel – *that* was why he was making a statement, not because he expected that 'so much as a single grain of truth would be ground out of the prayer wheels of justice'.

During the greater part of these preliminary remarks he spoke in dialect, and neither the judge nor the defence attorney, both of whom were sympathetic toward him, interrupted him or told him to speak up and not use dialect; the district attorney, who had often talked to Gruhl and neither liked nor understood the dialect, was not even bothering to listen; Herr Aussem, the court recorder and a junior barrister, was not taking down the statement at this stage: he found the trial a bore anyway. Among the spectators only two of Gruhl's friends understood even a few words of this rapid and toneless preamble, Frau Hermes and an elderly lady – one might almost say old – Fräulein Agnes Hall, an old friend of Gruhl's.

Gruhl then gave his occupation as cabinet-maker, his birth place as Dulbenweiler, Birglar County; he stated that he had attended elementary school there and graduated in 1929; that he had then been apprenticed in Birglar 'to my respected master, Herr Horn', and during his third year of apprenticeship had attended evening classes at the vocational school in the city; had gone into business for himself in 1936 at the age of twenty-one, married in 1937 at twenty-three, passed his master's examination in 1939 'at the minimum age' of twenty-five; that he had not been called up until 1940 and had remained a private until 1945.

Here for the first time the judge interrupted Gruhl's monotonous, barely audible statement, about which the court recorder later remarked that he had been continually forced to suppress an overpowering yawn; the judge asked the accused whether he had seen any actual fighting during the war or been politically active either before or during the war. Gruhl, in a gruff, almost inaudible voice – although firmly instructed by Dr Stollfuss to speak up – said that in answer to this he had much the same comment to make as about justice and the law; he had seen no actual fighting, nor had he been politically active, but – and here he raised his voice slightly as his annoyance became apparent – he would like to emphasize that this was due to neither heroism nor indifference: he simply had no time for that 'nonsense'. As far as his army years were concerned, he had been engaged chiefly as a cabinet-maker, making furniture for

18

officers' quarters and mess halls in 'what was to my mind their unmentionable taste', although his main job had been restoring 'stolen or confiscated furniture – Directoire, Empire, and at times Louis XVI' in occupied France and packing it suitably for shipment to Germany.

At this point the district attorney intervened with an objection to the term 'stolen' which, he said, tended to confirm or reawaken 'obsolete collective concepts of German barbarism'; moreover, the transport 'of French property from occupied France' had been prohibited both *de jure* and *de facto*; indeed, it had been subject to severe punishment. Gruhl looked at him calmly and repeated that he not only knew, he could swear – should an oath be required – that the greater part of the furniture had been stolen and, despite the ban – of which he was aware – sent to Germany, 'usually in the aircraft of highly decorated fellow sportsmen'; he couldn't care less, Gruhl added, whether he was expressing a collective opinion or not. As to his political activity: he had never taken much interest in politics, 'and certainly not in the nonsense' going on at that time; his deceased wife had been very religious and used to speak of the 'Anti-Christ'; he had been deeply attached to his wife, but had not understood this although he had respected it, and had 'almost revered her passionate feelings'; needless to say, he had always been 'on the side of the others', but that, he would like to emphasize, was to be *taken for granted*. After the war, with the help of Dutch friends – he had been in Amsterdam at the time – he had managed 'to avoid being taken prisoner by anybody', and from 1945 on he had once more lived and worked as a cabinet-maker in Huskirchen. The district attorney asked him what he meant by emphasizing the words *taken for granted*. Gruhl replied: 'You wouldn't understand.' The district attorney, somewhat piqued for the first time, objected to the accused expressing an opinion as to his intelligence. When reprimanded by Dr Stollfuss and instructed to reply to the district attorney, Gruhl said it was too involved and he refused.

When asked by the district attorney, whose temper was beginning to rise, whether he had ever been in conflict with the law, Gruhl said that during the last ten years he had lived in perpetual conflict with the law, the income tax law, but that he had not been previously convicted in the sense of the district attorney's question. On being told firmly to leave any opinion as to 'the sense of the district attorney's question' to the district attorney himself, Gruhl said he didn't want to be difficult and would admit that he had been constantly under property-seizure orders; Hubert was the one to testify about that. Gruhl, who was also beginning to get annoyed, explained in answer to the district attorney's question that Hubert was *Herr* Hubert Hall, the bailiff, a resident of Birglar, incidentally a cousin of his mother-in-law's father, if he might be permitted to be explicit. On being questioned by the defence attorney about his income and assets, Gruhl laughed pleasantly and asked to be allowed to leave the answering of that question, which was very, very complicated, to the witness Hall and the economist Dr Grähn.

His son, Georg Gruhl, a head taller and heavier than his father, on the stout side and fair-haired, did not at all resemble his father but was much like his deceased mother, so that many people believed they could 'instantly recognize her in him'. Lieschen Gruhl, née Leuffen, the daughter of a Huskirchen butcher, whose blonde hair and pale skin had been as famed as her piety and serene gentleness – who, known in the vernacular of the surrounding villages as 'Leuffen's Lies', was still spoken of in such lyrical terms as 'our golden angel', 'too good for this world', 'almost a saint' – had had only this one child. With what some spectators felt to be a rather excessive cheerfulness, Georg stated that he had attended elementary school in Huskirchen as far as fourth grade, then junior high school in Birglar, but since his early childhood had helped his father and, by arrangement with the guild, had passed his examination as cabinet-maker's apprentice simultaneously with graduating from junior high school, or, to be more precise, a few weeks later; for the next three years he had worked for his father and at twenty had been called up by the German Army; 'at the time when all this happened' he had been a private first class in the Bundeswehr. Furthermore, he subscribed to the explanatory remarks with which his father had preceded his statement.

The aspect of Gruhl's behaviour which the spectators felt to be a 'rather excessive cheerfulness' was described several times in a more private and somewhat literary section of Aussem's records as 'frivolous amusement'; it was in this tone that young Gruhl replied to some of the district attorney's questions. Had his imprisonment had an adverse mental effect on him, had it caused any damage perhaps? No, said young Gruhl, he had been glad to be with his father again after his military service, and since they had been given permission to work on small jobs he had even improved his skills; his father had also given him French lessons, and 'physically speaking' they had lacked for nothing.

Although the spectators were familiar with all this, in fact with almost more than the two Gruhls stated here in their matter-of-fact way, they appeared to be listening to these details very intently; and although the reading of the charges told them nothing they did not know, they listened to this too with great attentiveness.

One day in June 1965, the two Gruhls were found (here the judge corrected himself and said 'caught') on a path situated at an equal distance, i.e., just over a mile, from the villages of Dulbenweiler, Huskirchen, and Kireskirchen; the two men were sitting on a stone marker, smoking, and watching the German Army jeep burn to the ground; it later transpired that the younger Gruhl had been the driver. They were watching the fire not only 'with complete composure but with obvious satisfaction', according to the report of Inspector Kirffel of Birglar. The jeep's fuel tank, as Professor Kalburg, the arson specialist – who was reputed to be one of the most outstanding men in his field and whose evidence had had to be taken on commission – had stated in a written opinion, had first been pierced 'with a pointed steel object' and then, evidently at the scene of the crime, filled up with gasoline; moreover, the jeep 'must have had fuel poured all over it, in fact it must have been thoroughly soaked', for a mere burning of the tank's contents could not have caused such havoc as was later established. In view of this wanton perforation, as Professor Kalburg put it, an explosion could be regarded as virtually out of the question. In a surprisingly short time the 'considerable blaze' – although the Gruhls admitted to having carefully chosen a site, as noted above, about a mile from the surrounding villages, i.e., a 'relatively' lonely spot – had attracted a crowd of farmers and labourers from the near-by fields, schoolchildren returning from Huskirchen to the hamlets of Dulbenhoven and Dulbkirchen, but particularly motorists who, noticing the strange fire from the road, a second-class federal highway, had stopped to give assistance, satisfy their curiosity, or thrill to the sight of the 'considerable blaze'.

Upon being questioned, both the accused declared the report to be word-for-word accurate; they had nothing to add to it; some details of importance to them would emerge from the witnesses' statements. Urged by the judge to delay no longer in making the statement which they had refused in both preliminary and intermediate hearings, an explanation for this inexplicable deed, both men said, independently of each other, that their attorney would go into that in his pleadings. Did they not at least wish to contradict or qualify the terms 'with complete composure' and 'with obvious satisfaction', which could only be damaging to them? No, Inspector Kirffel had observed that very accurately and described it quite correctly. Did they plead guilty in the sense of the charges? 'In the sense of the charges, yes,' they both declared. The judge – now, contrary to his custom, beginning to show some irritation – asked whether he was to interpret this 'in the sense of the charges' as a qualification. Both the accused said yes, giving as their reasons the explanation that had preceded their statements.

Asked by the judge whether they felt any remorse, both men, without hesitation or qualification, answered, 'No.'

To the district attorney's request that they comment on the perforating of the fuel tank and clarify the still unanswered question as to which one had done the perforating and how, Gruhl senior replied that the arson specialist had ascertained that the perforating had been done with a pointed steel object, and he had nothing to add to this. When asked whether the two empty gasoline cans found at the scene had been the property of the Bundeswehr, the younger Gruhl replied yes, they had; one had formed part of the jeep's equipment, the other had been given him because he was starting out on a 'mission of some length'. Had he started out on this mission? Yes, he had, but he had interrupted it at home and 'then not resumed it'. It was the defence, not the prosecution, that asked Gruhl junior what type of mission it had been, but here the district attorney protested, saying he could not allow such a question to be put in public; he therefore requested that either the question be disallowed or the public excluded. The judge said he would like leave to put this question to Gruhl junior in the presence of his former superior officer, First Lieutenant Heimüller, who had been summoned as a witness; were the defence and the prosecution both agreeable to this? Both attorneys nodded their consent.

The evidence began with County Traffic Inspector Heuser, who had asked to be called first because he had to attend an important hearing, scheduled since the previous day, at which vital interests of the county were at stake. Heuser, a somewhat showily dressed, rather corpulent man with curly fair hair, who gave his age as twenty-nine and his profession as traffic sociologist, stated that 'a quarter of an hour after the probable time of the arson', i.e., about 12.45 p.m., a crowd of more than a hundred persons had gathered at the scene; a line of twenty-five parked motor vehicles had formed in the southbound lane and a line of forty motor vehicles in the northbound lane. The fact that the line-up facing north was longer by fifteen vehicles than the one facing south corresponded, as Heuser elaborately and somewhat complacently phrased it, 'precisely to the traffic data we have assembled in Birglar County and which is sufficiently known to the public as constituting a traffic crisis in our county', involving as it did a differential in the use of the highway surface. Heuser then went on to deal with another problem about which he seemed very much concerned: how to explain the phenomenon, observed for many years on this federal highway, of the 'north–south traffic imbalance', which amounted permanently to the figure of sixty per cent observed during the Gruhl affair; Heuser called the vehicles representing the

23

short-fall on the south–north return trip 'deviates' and 'vagrants' (which sounded like gypsies) and attributed this difference, which obviously distressed him, to the fact that, 'due to readily understandable sociological factors', a travelling salesmen's residential centre had grown up north of Huskirchen, and that they, the travelling salesmen, evidently used the federal highway to drive north but kept to the side roads on their return. He ignored the signal of the judge, who was trying to interrupt him, and, raising three fingers of his right hand as a warning to persons unknown, shouted: 'But I shall get to the bottom of this, I shall clear this matter up!' He had had the licence numbers of 'these gentlemen' taken down and was gathering data on the manner as well as the motives of this deviation or vagrancy, for a one-sided wear-and-tear hampered negotiations with the federal and provincial governments, which tried to lay the blame for it on rural conditions. At this point he finally paused in the presentation of his theory, a pause utilized immediately by the judge to ask him a simple, all-important question: had the action of the two accused impeded traffic? Heuser answered with a clear-cut, 'Of course, very much so.' Two accidents had occurred at the scene, he said: a small car had driven into a parked Mercedes 300 SL, the two drivers had come to blows, defamatory statements had been made; the Mercedes driver had spoken of a 'rabbit hutch', the small-car driver had referred – 'with your permission, Your Honour' – to a 'gas farter'. In addition he had observed that the drivers of a cement truck had made friends with the drivers of a beer truck, that exchanges of – 'I hope' – allowances in kind had been made on the spot, whether beer in exchange for cement or cement in exchange for beer was a point on which he did not wish to commit himself; but two days later he had seen the swamper of the beer truck, one Humpert from the hamlet of Dulbenhoven, repairing his driveway with cement made by that firm, while the two cement drivers had 'consumed the beer on the spot' and, two miles further on, had swerved off the highway and driven into a sugar-beet stack. There had been another collision between a drain-pipe truck and an Opel, seven drain pipes had – but here he looked suddenly at his watch, exclaimed in horror, 'Good heavens, the members of the legislature will be waiting,' and hastily begged leave to be excused. The judge raised his eyebrows at the defence and district attorneys; both shook their heads in resignation, and Heuser, still muttering 'traffic crisis' as he went, left the room. No one, least of all his wife, who was among the spectators, regretted Heuser's departure.

The evidence of the elderly Inspector Kirffel was short and to the point. He said that the scene of the crime was known to all local inhabitants for miles around as 'Küpper's Tree'; although there was no tree anywhere in the vicinity and never had been – not even in his childhood had he ever seen a tree there – he chose to use this name because it appeared on the regional maps. Herr Hermes, the teacher from Kireskirchen who was such an expert on local lore, had explained the name this way: some generations ago a tree had probably stood there, and someone called Küpper had either hanged himself or been hanged from it. What Heuser had been at such pains to describe he confirmed in a few sentences: the traffic jam, the two accidents, the scuffle, the exchange of insults; two charges of defamation were already pending, as well as compensation claims on the part of adjacent farmers for damage to their fields; fortunately no one had been injured in the collision between the drain-pipe truck and the Opel, but feelings had run high while he had been writing his report, for, on top of everything else, a passing cyclist, the farmer Alfons Mertens, had – 'of course not deliberately' – bounced a small piece of broken drain pipe with the rim of his back wheel against a factory-new, steel-blue Citroën, resulting in 'what I must admit was a very unsightly scratch' to its fender. Kirffel also confirmed the cement truck's collision with the sugar-beet stack, but stressed that it had been ascertained there had been no impaired driving; the accident was proved to have been caused by rotting sugar-beet leaves that had spread over on to the road after the stack had been opened. Kirffel several times used the word 'Patschkuhl', a local expression for sugar-beet stack, which had to be translated for the district attorney, recently transferred from Bavaria.

Kirffel, a grey-haired police officer who had grown ponderous with age and who among friends used the terms 'painful but unavoidable' in referring to the fact that, so shortly before his retirement and in what was probably his last case, he had to testify against the son and grandson of his old friend Gruhl; Kirffel, still very much the village policeman of the old school, went on to report that the jeep had finally almost burned itself out, it was just smoking and 'giving off sparks', which had prompted him to order the schoolchildren still further back. Meanwhile Schniekens and Tervel, the two police sergeants at the scene, had after some difficulty got the two lines of cars moving again; detained for the completion of the report, the only persons still at the scene were: the drivers of the Mercedes, the small car, the Opel, the Citroën, and the drain-pipe truck, and the farmer Alfons Mertens, but he had soon let the latter go since he was familiar with all his particulars. What had surprised Kirffel more than anything else, in fact had made him 'quite indignant', was the fact that the two Gruhls had not even tried to pretend it was an accident: on the contrary, they had admitted point-blank to having deliberately set fire to the jeep. It was at this juncture that Dr Hermes, the young attorney from Birglar, intervened for the first time; he asked Kirffel why he, an experienced police inspector, should have reckoned with the likelihood of a lie or an excuse, and was he, the defence attorney, to draw from this an inference that might come in handy later on in his career: that in such cases it was customary to lie, and perhaps the swift admission of his clients had been a lie? Before the astonished Kirffel, who of course had known Hermes since he was a toddler, and later referred to this question among his friends as 'unfair, but smart – he'll be a good attorney some day', before Kirffel, who from being deliberate had now become slow in his reactions, could reply, Dr Kugl-Egger, the district attorney, picked up the gauntlet and announced in sharp tones that he protested the attempt to defame a civil servant whose integrity and blameless political past were above suspicion. He could explain the witness's indignation very easily: to admit point-blank to such a shameful, indeed, destructive act, with no show of remorse and no attempt at extenuation, must arouse indignation in any right-thinking person. He, the district attorney – and he would take this up later in greater detail – regarded this 'bare-faced confession' as distinctly shocking, placing as it did the accused's frivolous attitude in the proper light. The defence attorney replied that right-thinking persons had not found the Gruhls' action at all shocking or criminal – rather more of a 'joke that had gone a bit too far', and he, the defence attorney, need hardly say that he had no intention whatever of defaming Kirffel, whom he respected and regarded as the very model of a civil servant. He had merely wanted to profit a little from Kirffel's many years of experience with the psychology of persons caught in the act.

At this point proceedings had to be interrupted because of a minor uproar. Calmly and without attracting attention, because 'nobody would believe his eyes', as it was expressed in Aussem's records, Gruhl senior had lighted his pipe and – as the record continued – smoked away 'in frivolous unconcern'. Schroer, the sheriff's officer, anxious to avoid a disturbance, tried to remove the pipe from Gruhl's hand; Gruhl resisted, instinctively rather than from any harmful intention, and snatched the pipe away, causing a burning flake of shag to land in the bosom of a lady sitting among the spectators. The lady, Frau Schorf-Kreidel, the youthful wife of the Mercedes 300 driver, had come merely, should the opportunity offer, to testify that since this 'Communist abuse' her husband had been suffering from a nervous complaint, as could be attested to by his doctor, Professor Fuhlbrock; that it had deeply affected her husband, whose progressive social views were well known and feared by radicals of every persuasion, to be abused by this fellow from Huskirchen, whose views were equally well known. Frau Schorf-Kreidel screamed, and this in turn prompted Gruhl to make a further startled movement, thereby scattering more flakes of glowing shag into the lap of another lady, burning a hole in her new silk dress; this lady also screamed, in short: there was a minor uproar, the proceedings had to be halted; a spectator dressed in his Sunday best, later identified as Leuffen, the Huskirchen butcher, Gruhl's brother-in-law, called out to the two accused men as he left the room the words commonly heard at village brawls, 'Attaboy, Johann, Georg, attaboy!'

Even after the short recess, the judge, who used it to telephone his wife and have a few puffs of his cigar, was not spared annoyance. As soon as the court was seated again, the lady with the damaged silk dress took it upon herself to stand up and ask the judge, whom she freely addressed as 'Alois', who was liable: the accused Gruhl, Schroer the sheriff's officer, the court, she herself, or her insurance company? What particularly annoyed the judge was the fact that, in using his first name – not, he surmised, without malice – she was publicly revealing a secret that had been carefully guarded in Birglar for many years, for to all who called him by his first name he was known as Louis; not even his wife remembered his real first name, of which he was very much ashamed.

This lady, his first cousin Agnes Hall, whose fine-drawn, virginal face had preserved a delicate beauty often denied married women of the same age, had been attending all his public trials for the past twenty years; she was known to everyone as 'Agnes, the court fixture'. In a more than independent position, financially speaking, she lived in an old patrician house in which Stollfuss's mother, a Hall, had been born, and in which Stollfuss had spent a great deal of time as a young man, an aspiring lawyer, and where he had often called to pick up Agnes for dances and other entertainment. The fact that she now transformed her mute reproach at his not having married her into this public exhibition of impertinence was completely misinterpreted by Stollfuss: he saw it as an example of outright and uncalled-for spite, whereas she – who had heard that morning by telephone that he was finally to be retired – all she wanted, since she would probably never meet him again, was to say good-bye, to have called him Alois just once more, a pleasure without meaning to those who did not understand platonic existences. Stollfuss, who was anyway becoming increasingly irritated, reacted with unexpected anger: he sternly instructed Agnes, whom – for the first time in his life or hers – he addressed as 'Fräulein Hall', that she must not speak in court without being asked to do so; that they were concerned here with the restitution of justice and not with everyday, trivial insurance matters. Knowing that it suited her, she assumed an expression of delicate mockery; then, as that seemed to have no effect since Stollfuss, speaking now in a much more official tone, carried on with his dry, severe admonition, Fräulein Hall began to show signs of mutiny: an offended twist to her shoulders, a rebellious pout to her lips; and when Stollfuss ordered her from the room she walked out proud and erect. There was an embarrassed silence as this handsome old woman 'swept' out of the room – the only way her exit could be described. Stollfuss watched her go, at first annoyed, then mortified; then he cleared his throat and recalled Inspector Kirffel to the witness-stand. More sharply than the elderly inspector deserved, he instructed him once and for all to omit everything that was not essential – the traffic jam and its consequences, the law infractions proceeding from it, the resultant civil claims and anticipated insurance squabbles. Kirffel, who had been much upset by the incident with Fräulein Hall, stated in a low voice that, after dealing with the various 'obstructions', he had immediately wanted to approach the accused, but at that moment the fire department had appeared on the scene, and it was only with the utmost difficulty that he had been able to prevent the firemen, who had already connected their pump to the near-by Duhr River, from 'bombarding' the slowly subsiding blaze with water, thus destroying possible clues and evidence; the fire department, 'offended, as usual on such occasions', had left, and at last he had been able to approach the accused. From some twenty feet away he had called out to them: 'Good God, what's happened?' The younger Gruhl had thereupon replied: 'We set fire to the thing.' Kirffel, somewhat surprised: 'But whatever for?' The older Gruhl: 'We felt a bit chilly and wanted to warm up with a Happening.' Kirffel: 'Hännchen – his father was one of my best friends, I've known the accused since he was a youngster and always call him Hännchen – d'you know what you're saying?' The older Gruhl: 'I know what I'm saying, it was a Happening.' Kirffel to the younger Gruhl: 'Georg – has Hännchen had one too many?'

Young Gruhl: 'No, Hennes – my first name's Heinrich, Your Honour – he hasn't been as sober as this for a long time.' Kirffel added that the entire conversation had taken place in dialect. Kirffel said later that this, his final testimony in court, must have been 'about the five hundredth in a trial conducted by Stollfuss,' and that it had been hard for him as well as for Stollfuss, so he had noticed, to keep strictly to the facts; for both of them, Stollfuss and he, in their 'usually vain efforts to instil a bit of order into this crazy world', had many a time fought on opposite sides where people were concerned but always on the same side where facts were concerned. How many times, Kirffel said, had he had to testify in court that his first name was Heinrich, which was why the accused addressed him as Hennes; he was sure he had made this statement alone two hundred times in court.

The defence attorney asked leave to put a few questions to the witness Kirffel; this granted, he said he would like to emphasize before putting the questions that it was not his intention to lay a trap for Kirffel, whom he respected and admired as a reliable police officer and an unimpeachable witness, or to cast doubt on his educational background or make him look ridiculous; Hermes blushed and stammered a little as he added that the questions were of crucial importance for his clients although they probably appeared trivial. He went on to ask Kirffel to explain to him and to the court his, Kirffel's, understanding of the expression 'Happening'. Kirffel, after first nodding to indicate that he did not regard this question as unfair, shook his head and said he hadn't really understood the expression but hadn't attached any significance to it. Later on he had thought about it and interpreted it roughly as follows: it was well known that Gruhl was always one for a joke and never had any cash, that since he was always being pursued by the bailiff he took every opportunity of emphasizing that he hadn't a penny; so Kirffel had taken this word 'Happening' to be garbled dialect form of 'haven't a penny', although even that hadn't explained the connection; he had simply regarded it as an unimportant variation of Gruhl's familiar lament about being broke.

He hadn't been able to connect it with the incident. When the defence attorney asked him how he would write or had written 'Happening', whether with one *p* or two, Kirffel replied that in his first report he hadn't mentioned the word at all, but if he had to he would of course write it with two *p*'s. The judge, who welcomed this diversion after the embarrassing incident with his cousin, followed the dialogue between Hermes and Kirffel with his eyebrows raised in interest. When Kirffel replied to the question about the spelling of the word 'Happening', the judge asked the defence attorney why he insisted on obtaining such an exact answer to a minor question of spelling; Hermes replied ominously that his questions were *not* intended to cast doubt on the credibility of the witness Kirffel, that was all he could say at this stage of the proceedings.

The district attorney followed this exchange about one *p* or two with a disdainful smile and murmured something about 'the hairsplitting of these pettifogging Rhinelanders' which was of no help at all. To him, and to the judge too, this seemed a time-wasting, trifling discussion about a dialect expression which he, the district attorney, considered ridiculously unimportant. In this – to his ears – thick, foreign dialect he had discovered a resemblance in some sounds to English, and the expression 'Happening' reminded him of the English pronunciation of 'halfpenny'. When the defence attorney asked that this one-*p*-two-*p* discussion be included in the record, a request that the judge granted with a smile, the district attorney laughed but at once became solemn again when he asked the accused whether he had been serious in claiming to have told the inspector at the scene of the incident that he had felt chilly or cold; after all, it had been a hot June day, and the temperature had been 84 degrees in the shade. Gruhl replied that he was always very cold when it was hot.

As was clearly apparent although not entered in the record, the defence attorney's second question caused Kirffel acute embarrassment: was it true, he asked, that the two Gruhls had been singing and knocking their pipes together, and had he, Kirffel, at 'this stage of the fire' heard the explosions reported by other witnesses? Kirffel, who obviously found it hard to lie, went red and looked beseechingly at Stollfuss, who in turn – as if asking for mercy for Kirffel – looked at Hermes. Hermes, clearly determined to treat Kirffel with great consideration, said that the answering of this question was of the utmost importance to his clients: in fact, in a 'favourable' sense, it had to do with his question about the spelling of 'Happening'; and if he, Kirffel, was concerned to spare the accused by saying nothing about these details, he, Hermes, could assure him to the contrary: his statement could only benefit the accused.

Here Gruhl senior asked leave to speak, was given permission, and told Kirffel, whom he addressed quite naturally as 'Uncle Hennes', not to distress himself or feel distressed; after such a long and blameless career he should make sure that his exit was a good one and speak 'openly'. Kirffel, who later described this scene as 'highly embarrassing', said, as he groped for words, yes, he had observed the two accused knocking their pipes together, and he had heard them singing. When asked whether the pipes had been knocked together rhythmically, Kirffel said, speaking a little more freely now, yes, it had been rhythmic – for forty years, as they all knew, he had been in the church choir and was familiar with liturgical chants – the pipes had been knocked together in time to the *Ora pro nobis*, often enough, in fact, for him to have been able to recognize it unmistakably as he approached the Gruhls; it had only stopped when he had called out his first question to Gruhl – and, added Kirffel, now showing some embarrassment again: only the younger Gruhl had been singing – in a low, almost inaudible voice Kirffel went on to say that he had recognized the All Saints' Litany. In fact they must have been quite far along in it; when he came close to them they had got as far as St Agatha and St Lucia; he had 'not been in time to hear' the explosions; they had only been noticed and reported by the very first ones on the scene, the travelling salesman Erbel from Wollershoven near Huskirchen, and the schoolboys Krichel and Boddem from Dulbenhoven. Hermes thanked Kirffel with marked cordiality. The district attorney asked Kirffel only one question: whether 'all this non-

sense', about which Kirffel, a sensible man, naturally found it
hard to testify, had been reported. Kirffel said the statements of
the two boys Krichel and Boddem had been taken down, and as
far as he knew the witness Erbel was to be questioned on the
subject.

In a low voice, courteous but firm, the district attorney now
pointed out to the judge that His Honour had possibly over-
looked reprimanding Gruhl for smoking on the witness bench.
Dr Stollfuss accepted this reminder with thanks, requested
Gruhl senior to approach the rail, and asked him with paternal
severity to explain what he had had in mind when he calmly
lighted his pipe; he was not – regardless of whatever would be
proved against him – he was not a discourteous man, let alone
an insolent one. Gruhl, who remained serious and dignified,
begged to be excused for this incident. He hadn't had anything
in mind; on the contrary he hadn't been thinking about his pipe
at all, he had been absent-mindedly thinking of something else;
he had not intended any disrespect for the court. His mind had
been on a little job he had been allowed to undertake while in
custody – the staining and restoring of a small Directoire jewel
case of rosewood from which the clasp and hinges were missing.
These must have been of gold and had been removed and replaced at the turn of the century by unsightly copper fittings;
he had suddenly had to think of his work, and whenever he
thought of his work he would reach for his pipe, fill it, and light
it. When asked whether he was able to follow something as
important to him as this trial while absent-mindedly thinking of
something else, Gruhl said he had indeed been thinking of
something else but perhaps absent-minded was not the proper
word; he was quite capable of being aware of his surroundings
and at the same time thinking of something else; it had even
happened – as Father Kolb from his own village of Huskirchen
could verify – that he had started to smoke in church. Gruhl
then turned round briefly toward the spectators and apologized
to the two ladies who had suffered from his carelessness and
declared his readiness to make good the damage – if necessary,
should he lack the cash, by working for them; he had often done

jobs for Frau Schorf-Kreidel as well as for Fräulein Hall. Gruhl spoke quietly and matter-of-factly, but with no trace of servility, until the district attorney, this time more sharply than ever, interrupted him and said he regarded the manner in which the accused was publicly offering his services as a kind of cleverly understated advertising, a fresh proof of his 'frivolous amusement and unconcern which I must emphatically demand be punished at the very least by a severe reprimand in the name of the state, concerned here with the restoration of justice'. In a voice that failed to carry much conviction, Dr Stollfuss delivered a severe reprimand to Gruhl senior, which the latter acknowledged with a nod. Gruhl returned to the witness bench where he was observed to hand over pipe, tobacco pouch, and matches to Schroer, the sheriff's officer, who was sitting beside him and who received these three articles with a nod of approval.

Kirffel could now finish giving his evidence. He had, he said, immediately arrested both Gruhls, and was surprised when they went along not only without resisting but almost cheerfully; he had hesitated a few moments, but Gruhl senior had called out that they intended to escape to Paris or Amsterdam and that they were therefore under suspicion of trying to run away. Even then, not being quite clear as to the legal position, he still hesitated to arrest the younger Gruhl, who was in uniform; but since Gruhl junior did not resist he felt justified in standing in for the military police until the legal position was clarified. The district attorney's interjection of 'Very good' obviously embarrassed Kirffel. The district attorney was rebuked by the judge for his interjection, which had been neither permitted nor relevant; this was not the place, the judge said, for public demonstrations of approval. The district attorney apologized but explained that, in view of the latent frivolity apparent in both the accused, he had wished to show his approval of the deserving police officer's conscientious behaviour and presence of mind.

At the defence attorney's request, the legal position of Gruhl junior was once again carefully examined. The morning after his arrest, the younger Gruhl had been called for by his unit and taken to a detention cell, interrogated by his superior officer, but released that same afternoon, and then transferred in civilian clothes by the military police to the Birglar jail. He would still have to clarify the question of whether Gruhl's unit had been entitled to have a remand prisoner who had been categorically declared a civilian conveyed by the military police to Birglar; but his present concern was to establish whether Gruhl junior was now finally before the court as a civilian or whether he was liable to further proceedings. The judge stated that at first the legal position had not been quite clear: the younger Gruhl's offence had first been regarded as having been committed while on active service; but then, when the question was raised whether Gruhl senior had not also committed a crime against the Bundeswehr, it had been established in the company office of Gruhl's unit that, due to a miscalculation, or rather a wrong entry in the furlough records, Gruhl had actually been due for discharge three days before the incident. At the time of the incident, therefore, he had belonged, subjectively but no longer objectively, to the Bundeswehr, and similarly had been, subjectively but no longer objectively, entitled to drive the jeep; Gruhl ought to look on this as a great concession, for, had the incident been found to be sabotage, he would have been liable to very serious proceedings. In this case, however, the Bundeswehr was not appealing as an injured party and in any event regarded Gruhl senior as the chief perpetrator; the Bundeswehr, said Dr Stollfuss with a rather sour smile, 'was washing its hands in innocence'. It was not joined as a plaintiff and was represented by some of its members as a 'witness' only. Moreover, the affair was only to be judged in conjunction with Gruhl's aforementioned mission; the military aspects of the case would be discussed later as soon as Lieutenant Heimüller gave his evidence and the public was excluded. Of one thing he could assure the defence attorney: Gruhl would not have to face a second trial; as far as damages were concerned, the Bundeswehr would look to the Gruhls as civilians via the County Court of Birglar. A letter to this effect had been received from the regimental commander, Colonel von Greblothe. The younger Gruhl, whose request for permission to speak was granted, said he was not interested in the Bundeswehr making him a gift of anything, even legal proceedings. The district attorney quickly turned on him and shouted that he was an ungrateful young punk. Gruhl junior shouted back that he would not tolerate being called a young punk; he was an adult and it was up to him to decide whether to accept a gift or not; he would say it again, he refused to accept even being spared legal proceedings as a gift. The district attorney was ordered to withdraw the expression 'young punk', and Gruhl was warned against unruly behaviour; both apologized, but not to each other, only to the judge.

Albert Erbel, travelling salesman, resident of Wollershoven near Huskirchen, Birglar County, gave his age as thirty-one; he stated that he was married, with two children and 'two dogs', as he facetiously added; the judge forbade him to repeat such gratuitous jokes. Yes, said Erbel, after apologizing, on the day in question he had been driving past that particular spot at about 12.35 p.m., had noticed the fire, stopped, and turned his car – this later made it difficult for him to drive on again in his original direction. He had then run up toward the burning vehicle, 'about fifty yards away', had seen the two men knocking their pipes together – 'you know, the way you clink beer glasses for a toast' – and singing; he hadn't been able to make out what they were singing, but yes, it might have been Latin, 'not German anyway, and not dialect – that I understand'. When asked about the explosions, Erbel said yes, that had sounded very queer, 'beautiful, in a way', more like a kind of drumming or rattling, in any event it had sounded like small objects being violently shaken inside a metal container; it had had, if he recalled it correctly, a sort of rumba rhythm. Well anyway, he had asked the two men if there was anything he could do for them; no, they had said, it was up to them to do something for him, he should 'take a good look and listen', didn't he find it pleasing? For answer he had tapped his forehead and gained the distinct impression that the two men were crazy, or that it was a 'hoax, though rather an expensive one, I must say, for the taxpayer', and had returned to his car. When asked by the defence attorney whether he had thought the two men were crazy or were *acting* crazily, Erbel considered for a few seconds and said he had thought they were *acting* crazily; did he, continued Hermes, feel that he was witnessing a haphazard occurrence, an accident, or a planned event? Erbel: He certainly had not thought it haphazard or accidental, and the expression 'planned event' did not seem quite the right one under the circumstances, although 'fairly close'; in any case – this much he had realized – it had been a *calculated* affair. When reminded by the district attorney that his statement at the preliminary hearing had covered considerably more ground, Erbel slapped his forehead, apologized, and said, yes, now he remembered: Gruhl junior had asked him what he was selling or what firm he represented. He had told him he travelled for a well-known manufacturer of bath oil; Gruhl had then asked him for a sample bottle or tube, but he had refused; then Gruhl had said he was going to buy a bottle of the stuff, the jeep needed a bath.

The two accused men confirmed Erbel's evidence as being 'word-for-word' correct. Erbel then described the difficulty he had had in turning his car and getting back into his original direction; by this time there had been about ten vehicles parked there: Sergeant Schniekens had helped him to back up into a field.

The district attorney, the newcomer who had been in office for only a week, made a cardinal mistake in his effort to throw an unfavourable light on the character of Gruhl senior. Only a few minutes before the trial opened, the judge had urged the district attorney not to call Sanni Seiffert as a witness; but the district attorney, suspecting some local corruption, had insisted on being allowed to interrogate her about the accused. Actually, in summoning Sanni Seiffert, Dr Kugl-Egger, had succumbed to the innuendoes of a Social Democrat editor of the *Rhineland Daily News,* who was subsequently not only not praised by his party for making these innuendoes but sharply criticized and almost kicked out. Frau Seiffert, the editor had assured him, would testify at any time that on several occasions Gruhl senior had tried to assault her.

The witness 'Frau Sanni Seiffert' was now called, and upon

the sheriff's going out into the corridor and shouting into the witness-room, with no pretence at formality and loud enough for everyone in the courtroom to hear, 'Come along, Sanni dear, your hour has struck,' a certain malicious glee spread among most of the spectators, obviously at the expense of the district attorney. The entrance of the witness, a pretty, smartly dressed woman no longer in her first youth, with very dark dyed hair and wearing bright red-leather boots, embarrassed the judge. On several occasions he had had dealings with Frau Seiffert in connection with receiving stolen goods, procuring, and corrupting minors, and for the activity generally known as 'sexual intercourse' she commanded a whole arsenal of dialect expressions that had sometimes brought blushes to the cheeks of the most seasoned authorities. Moreover, he had twice had to interrogate her in connection with suspected espionage, but this had proved unfounded. Frau Seiffert had merely had very intimate relations with the American officer who held the key to the atomic warheads at the airfield, which was closer to Birglar than to the neighbouring city; she had also associated very intimately with a Belgian major who had access to classified information, but in both cases she had been able to prove that her intentions had been simply those customary in her profession. During her brief appearance her blue eyes became increasingly clear and hard, proving them to be the eyes of a person who was extremely blond by nature and of a quite definite disposition; and she surveyed all the men present, with the exception of the accused and the district attorney, with contemptuous defiance. The judge did not permit himself to smile when she gave her occupation as restaurant proprietress and her age as 'twenty-eight'. The district attorney – who had realized his mistake as soon as she entered the courtroom, cursed the innuendoes of the Social Democrat editor, and made up his mind *not* to vote for that party at the next election – now asked Frau Seiffert in uncertain tones whether she had ever been molested by the accused Gruhl or whether he had attempted to assault her. The defence attorney immediately jumped to his feet and requested, not, as he explicitly stated, in the interests of his client Gruhl senior, who

38

had nothing to fear from the witness's evidence, but in the interests of public decency and morality the safeguarding of which was actually not his task but the district attorney's – he requested that not only the public be excluded but also his youthful client Gruhl junior; his agitation as he shouted that he found it positively monstrous the way the representative of public morality was trying to blacken a father in his son's eyes sounded sincere. Before the district attorney could decide to answer, Frau Seiffert said in a surprisingly gentle voice that it was her job to be molested by men, she was – the judge interrupted her brusquely to point out that she only had to answer when she was asked a question, whereupon she said, raising her voice, that she had been asked a question and that she had merely replied. Meanwhile the district attorney had looked at his wife among the spectators, a slender dark person whom only the defence attorney's wife knew to be the wife of the district attorney; his wife had indicated to him by a look that he should not insist on Frau Seiffert's testifying, and when the judge now asked him whether he insisted on Frau Seiffert's evidence, he announced in a low voice that he would dispense with any further testimony on her part. The judge did not look at Frau Seiffert as he politely gave her to understand that she was dismissed. Frau Seiffert, her gentleness become brittle, then asked whether, in order not to leave Gruhl senior under false suspicion, she might not reply at least to the second part of the question; upon the judge's indicating by a reluctant nod that she might do so, she said Gruhl senior had never tried to molest her, let alone assault her; he had merely done some work for her, fixed up her bar in *fin de siècle* style – which she pronounced correctly – and naturally the workmen she employed came easily under suspicion of having business relations with her of a kind other than those actually existing; furthermore, Gruhl junior had also done some work for her and she had enjoyed cooking for the two 'orphaned' men. By the time she left the room as instructed, her voice was on the verge of that condition commonly known as 'choking with tears'. A kind of applause became audible in the courtroom, a shifting of chairs and some sounds that, although not articulated, obviously indicated acclamation and were suppressed by the judge. The appearance of Frau Seiffert, who was to be seen shortly afterward on the former playground getting into her red sports car and driving off, ended in an awkward silence, the awkwardness of which was not diminished by Aussem's going over to the judge and asking him in a whisper whether he was to record this incident as an 'uproar'; annoyed, because the whisper was clearly audible throughout the room, the judge shook his head.

A none too discreet knock at the door startled Schroer, who jumped up, ran across, and from the door called back to the judge that the witness Detective Commissioner Schmulck had just arrived and was ready to testify. The judge asked for him to be shown in. In response to a request, Schmulck, in civilian clothes, youthful, a 'bouncy intellectualistic type', supplied a few hitherto unknown details: the perpetrator – despite repeated efforts it had been impossible to establish whether the younger or the older Gruhl – had thrown, 'from a safe distance', a previously ignited 'small detonator such as was usually on sale at carnival time' into the gasoline-soaked jeep, with the immediate desired result; even the tyres had been meant to burn, and although two tyres had withstood the blaze, the effects of the heat had caused them to explode. Apart from the burned-out wreck, the only clues were the charred remains of firecracker-like objects in the jeep's fuel tank and two reserve jerry cans; all that had been found – some twelve feet from the wreck on the adjacent sugar-beet field – had been the cardboard container of the detonator, a brand sold as 'Cannonball'. He testified that during the interrogation the accused had been, if not precisely obstinate, not very loquacious; they had insisted that they had carried out the deed 'jointly', yet only one of them could have ignited the detonator, only one of them could have thrown it into the jeep. The wreck, after being searched for clues by experts, had been claimed by the Bundeswehr and towed away; however, as was unavoidable, all detachable parts had been removed by the youthful inhabitants of the near-by hamlet of

Dulbenhoven; the speedometer had stood at 2,994 miles. When asked by the judge whether there was any point in having the site inspected, Schmulck replied, no, none whatever; at the end of the summer he had found some matches next to the stone marker, as well as a tobacco tin of American manufacture, which he had identified as belonging to the accused, but the start of the sugar-beet harvest which, of course, required the use of heavy vehicles, had 'completely churned up' the immediate area, leaving nothing more to be seen there. He glanced at his watch and with business-like politeness asked to be excused as he was to testify in the early afternoon in the city at the trial of the child murderer Schewen, who had also, 'fortunately without success', been active in Birglar County. Neither the district nor defence attorney had any objection to Schmulck's dismissal.

Prosecution and defence had each summoned two psychiatrists to give expert opinions; of each of these pairs, one was a university professor and one was not; a further counterbalance, eliminating both controversy and inequality in the trial of the accused, was the fact that the professor called by the defence belonged to a school to which the non-professor called by the prosecution belonged, a school which carried on a constant and even public controversy with the school to which the professor called by the court and the non-professor called by the defence belonged. This unusual arrangement had earned high praise from 'down there' for the judge, who had been at enormous pains to engineer it; it was later to be extolled and recommended among legal experts as the 'Stollfuss model'. Thus Birglar, where it was first successfully applied, and the two Gruhls were to go down in legal history. Since the psychiatrists had had ample opportunity to interview the accused while they were in remand custody, the judge, after receiving the consent of defence and prosecution, had excused them from appearing personally in court on account of the distances involved – they lived respectively in Munich, Berlin, and Hamburg – and a judge had been requested to take their evidence.

Dr Stollfuss said that the contents of their written opinions were known to all parties and, as far as the particulars relating to the accused were concerned, they contained nothing that had not already been said. He could therefore dispense with reading the full texts and confine himself to stating that all four experts, independently of one another and despite the fact that they belonged to conflicting schools, had arrived unanimously at the opinion that both the accused were of above-average intelligence, were fully responsible for their actions, had been found to have neither psychic nor mental defects, and that their action was attributable – uncommon though this was – to conscious rather than emotional impulses; it was possibly even a case of *Homo ludens* expressing himself in a manner which, though legally culpable, corresponded to the personalities of the accused, both being of a decidedly artistic temperament. Only one of the psychiatrists, Professor Herpen, had found in Gruhl senior – he was now quoting verbatim, the judge said – 'a certain, I would not say minimal but not very considerable, emotionally-conditioned trauma of the social consciousness, possibly the result of the premature death of his beloved wife'. All four psychiatrists had unanimously and categorically denied that pyromania might have been the cause of the accused's behaviour. It was therefore clear, the judge went on, from the testimony of all four experts that this had been an act of will; the impulses had come from neither the subconscious nor the unconscious, and this fact became clear when one reflected that the two accused had committed the deed jointly, although they were so different in disposition and character. When the judge asked whether there were any more questions on the subject of 'psychiatric testimony', the district attorney said he required no further expert opinion, he was satisfied with the establishment of full responsibility and with the designation 'act of will' for the deed, but he would like to be sure that the definition 'respectable character', which occurred several times in the statements, was understood to be a medical rather than legal definition. The defence attorney asked leave to read aloud the passage in which the 'artistic temperament of both the accused' was mentioned. On receiving the judge's permission, the defence attorney read aloud what was, as he pointed out, almost identical in all four statements, namely Gruhl senior's 'astonishing ability to recognize, reflect, and reproduce styles', and Gruhl junior's rather more artistic gift which had already expressed itself 'in various wood sculptures and non-representational paintings'. Courteously, almost cordially, the defence attorney was now asked by the judge whether he cared to call for a further expert opinion so that, in view of the baffling nature of the offence, the accused might not be entirely deprived of the chance of being found not responsible for their actions. After a brief whispered consultation with his two clients, the defence attorney politely declined the offer.

Upset and nervous as he was, Dr Stollfuss (he had also known Gruhl senior from childhood and had always had a soft spot for him – a few weeks before the incident he had even employed him to restore a valuable Empire chest of drawers which had finally, after a lengthy inheritance dispute with his cousin Lisbeth, a sister of Agnes Hall, come into his possession. In paying Gruhl he had in fact, if not demonstrably, put himself in the wrong because, knowing that Gruhl was being snowed under with seizure orders, he had 'slipped him his money privately') Dr Stollfuss forgot to declare the noon recess and just before one o'clock gave instructions to summon the witness Erwin Horn, master of the carpenters' guild.

Herr Horn, neatly and respectably attired, with white hair and an air of florid joviality, could very well have passed for a retired church dignitary. He gave his age as seventy-two, his residence as Birglar, and stated that he had known the accused, who had served his apprenticeship with him, for thirty-five years; he had been a member of the commission when Gruhl had passed his journeyman's exam with 'very good'; when Gruhl had taken his master's exam he had ceased, for political reasons, to be a member of the commission. Horn, who without seeming aggressive was endowed with a distinctly youthful *élan*, gave his testimony in a clear, lively voice. He said Gruhl had always been a quiet boy, and a quiet man too; not only had he shared his political sympathies, but during the war when he, Horn, had been exposed to considerable economic pressure by those 'dirty crooks', Gruhl had always stood by him. For example, he had brought him butter, bacon, eggs, and tobacco from France, and Gruhl's wife Lieschen had always kept him supplied with milk and potatoes – in short, Gruhl had never tried to hide his sympathy for him, although he had never been politically active. Horn was also full of praise for Gruhl's professional ability; it was hard to find a cabinet-maker of his calibre, and his skills placed him among a dying race of craftsmen – in fact, he was a rarity. Horn could not resist pointing out that in the course of the last forty-five years of German history several carpenters had risen to the highest positions in the land, one even becoming head of state. When the judge asked him whom he meant, since so far as he knew Ebert had been a saddler and Hitler a house-painter, Horn became embarrassed and tried to extricate himself by a grammatical hairsplitting, saying that what he had meant was *become*, not *been*, head of state, and anyway – he certainly didn't want to cast aspersions on the profession of house-painter, for Hitler hadn't even been a proper house-painter, in other words his remarks did not apply to any colleague of this guild – anyway Hitler couldn't conceivably have been a *carpenter*. Here the district attorney intervened, saying that, before the witness continued with his eulogies and before he managed to cover up the outrageous things he had just said by means of a totally unacceptable flight of historical fancy, he, the district attorney, would like to register the strongest possible objection 'to the Soviet Zone being spoken of, here in a German court of law and without protest, as a state'; no German court could tolerate this. He demanded that the witness Horn be reprimanded and that the accused Gruhl senior, whose face was once more registering 'frivolous amusement', again be instructed to show respect for the court. The judge, now for the first time grasping which head of state was meant, murmured 'Oh, I see'; he acknowledged that he had not known that 'that fellow' was or had been a carpenter, duly administered the reprimand to the witness Horn in clearly unenthusiastic tones, and instructed Gruhl senior to abstain from his 'frivolous attitude'. When asked about the accused's financial circumstances, Horn replied that for the last ten years these had been 'habitually deplorable', but he would like to emphasize strongly that the blame for this was not only Gruhl's, who had never been very good at figures and was probably a bit easy-going with money; the blame also lay with 'a ruinous policy toward the middle classes'. Once again the district attorney interrupted to say he could not, as representative of the state, permit the trial to be misused for propaganda against the government's tax policy, but the judge quietly pointed out that it was perfectly in order to refer to the accused's subjective situation within the framework of an objective context, even when this context was expressed in popular terms. With obvious satisfaction Horn then proceeded to embark on details; he could not, he said, disclose each and every circumstance, that was up to a financial expert; because Gruhl had not been able to cope with the numerous categories – turnover tax, business tax, income tax, professional dues, and health insurance – he had got into arrears; these arrears had been increased, in fact compounded, by property seizures; these had been followed by forced sales. First the Gruhl family home in Dulbenweiler, then two fields and a meadow near Kireskirchen that he had inherited from his godmother, and finally his share in the inn, the Jug of Beer, in Birglar, part of his inheritance from his mother, had come under the hammer; meanwhile, he had also been robbed of his entire attachable furniture, including some very valuable pieces of which two had already reappeared in the local museum. An attempt by the district attorney to object to the term 'robbed' for a legitimate procedure on the part of the state was brushed aside by the judge with a gesture. He would dispense, Horn went on, with further details, he would merely confine himself to saying that the accused's financial situation – he was ignoring the question of blame, he was simply stating the position – had been as confused as it was confusing. In the end it had come to 'personal search and seizure'; Gruhl had finally lost interest in large orders; he had also lost his best customers, who might

45

have had reason to fear complications. Gruhl had earned his living by working 'under cover', and finally – 'he was in a natural state of self-defence' – took payment in kind only, this being very hard to seize. Vehemently, almost abusively, the district attorney objected to the expressions 'natural' and 'self-defence' – he simply could not allow these expressions, as applied by the witness to the accused's behaviour, to pass; the expression 'self-defence' struck him as particularly subversive, positively outrageous; no citizen, if he obeyed the law, could ever find himself in a condition of self-defence as against the state. The judge, whose calm demeanour appeared to inflame the district attorney's wrath, pointed out how many citizens, both past and present, had made themselves liable to prosecution not by obeying the law but by *not* obeying, and had thus practised a type of self-defence that had been the only humanitarian course; in a democracy the expression 'self-defence' was of course 'somewhat exaggerated', and he requested Horn to try and avoid the phrase. As for the word 'natural', he could not really find fault with it; to take a stand on this presupposed a detailed definition of what was known as human nature, and under no circumstances could any citizen of any state regard tax legislation and its consequences as 'natural'; a man with the experiences of Herr Horn, whose integrity was well known and who had had to endure scorn and persecution on this account, was perfectly entitled to describe the accused's behaviour as 'natural'. Indeed, by their very intention justice and the law were directed *against* what was assumed to be human nature, and it was too much to expect every citizen to regard all the procedures taken against him as 'natural'. Stollfuss, who was in danger of lapsing into a somewhat sleepily delivered sermon, was woken here by the defence attorney loudly clearing his throat. The two men had privately agreed on this signal for such occasions. Stollfuss broke off in the middle of a sentence and asked Horn whether a man of Gruhl's ability could not very well earn his living without getting into difficulties. Horn admitted that this was possible, but the way things were today it was almost, he emphasized the almost, necessary to have some training in economics or at least an awareness of the subject; this financial instruction, this forming of a financial awareness, and an initiation into all the various dodges, were things that the guild not only strove to achieve but offered to its members in the form of courses and circulars; however, Gruhl had never taken part in these courses and lectures and had never read the circulars. He had – and this was only natural, for his situation had already reached the point where instruction would not have been much use – buried his head in the sand and had begun not to keep account of payments received, quite large payments; this had come to light in various audits and had led to severe tax penalties. In such cases – and there were more of them than might be imagined, in other professions too – the only course for a man in that position was 'to go into industry and submit to seizure orders for the rest of his natural days', and it was just this 'going into industry' that Gruhl had refused to do; he was even offered a good job as head of a carpentry department in a well-known firm of interior decorators, but he had turned it down, saying he was a free man and wanted to remain one. When asked whether the disaster had not been avoidable, Horn said: 'Avoidable, yes, Your Honour, but by the time you're in the mess Johann Gruhl was in, this doesn't help you any more. There's simply no way out; just think of the costs arising out of the seizures, the interest, fees, and incidentals – it'd be the death of you.' With a gentle smile the judge made it clear that he was not to be addressed with quite so much familiarity.

The district attorney, not without bitter irony and a sense of injury, said he would like to ask leave, 'with that humility required from me here as representing the state', to interrupt the witness Horn in his moving description of the accused's martyrdom and ask a few questions. He would refrain from asking for a censure of the phrase 'all the various dodges', which lowered tax legislation to the level of some sort of sleight of hand, in fact was an outright defamation; he would refrain from doing this, he merely wished to ask the witness whether he had known of the accused's book-keeping irregularities before these were discovered. Horn admitted without hesitation, yes, he had known about them, Gruhl had had complete confidence in him and told him everything. How was it then that the witness had not seen himself compelled to inform the authorities? Horn, managing to suppress his anger, said that as master of the guild he was not an informer for the income tax department, and not only was he not an informer for the income tax department, he was 'not an informer, period'; the district attorney should realize, if he might be permitted to make such a suggestion, that a guild represented a community of interests of fellow workers. He had urged Gruhl, strongly advised him in fact, to set his affairs in order, had even succeeded in persuading the income tax department to consider a settlement to help his colleague regain terra firma and the desire to work; it had looked as though the department was going to cooperate, but just then Gruhl's son, who had been a good support to him, had been called up, and as a result Gruhl's situation had taken a turn for the worse. From then on Gruhl had done just enough work to preserve his house in Huskirchen from a forced sale and to be able to take care of his light bill and essential materials. Since then Gruhl had struck him as being resigned, and there was one thing he wanted to emphasize again most strongly: he was not an informer, nor was he born to be an informer. Upon being told by the judge to withdraw the word 'informer' in the context of the district attorney's question, Horn refused; he said the challenge to inform on a colleague had been all too plain. Once more urged, then firmly but kindly instructed not to land himself in difficulty and to withdraw the word, Horn said no, during his lifetime – before 1933, after 1933, and after 1945 – he had attended a total of more than three dozen trials, and he refused to withdraw the word 'informer'. He was promptly sentenced to a fine of fifty marks payable to the public treasury, and upon being asked whether he accepted the penalty he replied that, if it was so expensive to tell the truth, he would gladly pay this sum although personally he would prefer to be allowed to pay it into the workers' welfare fund. Stollfuss's tone sharpened as he demanded that Horn withdraw this new insult to the court. Since Horn indicated his refusal by an obstinate shake of the head, he was fined a further seventy-five marks payable to the public treasury. He was not asked this time whether he accepted the penalty; the judge declared a noon recess of an hour and a half, and declared the witness Horn dismissed.

Two

Bergnolte, the slight, quietly but well-dressed middle-aged man who had been sitting in the courtroom as a silent observer, had inconspicuously left the room ten minutes before the judge announced the noon recess. As soon as he reached the playground he quickened his pace, after a glance at his wrist-watch stepped out even more hurriedly, and by the time he reached the nearest public telephone booth, by the east chancel of the Birglar parish church, he was moving at a surprisingly well coordinated run from which one might have judged him to be an athlete in his spare time. In the telephone booth, not out of breath but breathing rapidly, he tipped open his black change purse on to the little shelf, some of the coins bouncing off the telephone directory and rolling on to the floor, from which he picked them up. After a slight hesitation, he decided to use the ten-pfennig pieces first but to keep larger coins in readiness; he dropped the seven ten-pfennig pieces he had selected one by one into the appropriate slot, observing rather wistfully how his coins piled up one behind the other in the slanting groove inside the apparatus; this reminded him of a similar process in those pinball games he had so often played in his youth (most of them being in taverns, which he was forbidden to enter). Again, this time successfully, he deposited two coins that had been rejected, smiling as the word 'rejected' went through his mind, dialled four prefix numbers, then six more, groped for the larger coins with his right hand while he waited for the voice of Grellber's secretary, put them back into his open change purse, did the same with the five-pfennig coins, and was beginning to arrange the remaining fifty-pfennig and one-mark pieces into little piles when the girl's voice he had been waiting for at last came through. 'Hello,' he said quickly, almost conspiratorially, 'Bergnolte speaking'; the girl plugged in so that her 'One moment, please' reached his ears as a mutilated 'One mo'; a man's voice said 'Grellber speaking' and erased the gruff official tone as soon as Bergnolte mentioned his name again: 'Fire away!'

'Well,' said Bergnolte, 'things are moving a bit slowly, but quite nicely, from your point of view, I mean.'

'Which is yours too, I hope.'

'That goes without saying. No reporters, the usual local colour, enough to amuse and provoke our friend Stollfuss; generally speaking: no danger!'

'How about the new man?'

'A bit over-zealous, confused too because he's new to the place – now and again makes a fool of himself. He could do with a polite little damper, not because he's actually in the wrong, but because he introduces too many political, I mean legal-political, factors and we can't have that.'

'And Hermes?'

'First class. He's clever enough to hide the inevitable lawyer's demagogy under his Rhineland accent and an unfailing deference toward Stollfuss and the witnesses. Sometimes gets bogged down splitting hairs. The difference between one p and two is hardly going to save his clients.'

'What do you mean?'

'A bit of fun I'll explain to you this evening.'

'What do you think – should I nudge Stollfuss?'

'Just try and make him hurry up a bit, but be careful. He's really magnificent – but if he allows the remaining eleven witnesses to talk that long, he'll need four more days.'

'Good – stay right there, will you; we'll talk it over tonight.'

'How's the Schewen case going?'

'Oh, nothing new – he's wallowing in his confession, just like the Gruhls.'

'There's no wallowing about their confession.'

'What would you call it then?'

'Oh, an absolutely staggering casualness.'

'Fine – tell me about it this evening – good-bye.'

'Good-bye.'

Bergnolte swept the rest of his change over the edge of the shelf into his purse and, as he replaced the receiver, was startled when two of his seven coins came clattering out of the slanting groove into the coin scoop; he removed these two as well, left the booth, and walked slowly round the church toward the main street of Birglar, where after a short search he found what had been recommended to him as the best restaurant in town, the Duhr Terraces. He was quite hungry, his appetite sharpened by the prospect of an expense-account meal, something that did not often come his way. In hopes of sunny autumn weather, a few white tables had been left out on the terrace above the river; the tables were covered with early autumn leaves, stuck to the surface by persistent rain. Bergnolte was the first midday guest; in the quiet, dark-panelled dining-room, an old-fashioned stove emanated a comforting warmth that seemed to him a token of traditional hospitality. Of the twenty or so tables, fifteen were laid for lunch; on each table stood a freshly picked rose in a slender vase. After taking off his coat, hat, and scarf, Bergnolte, rubbing his hands, went across to a table in the window with a view over the Duhr, a little river which the local inhabitants did not like to hear called a stream, flowing between tired, damp, autumnal meadows toward a distant power plant. The Duhr was in flood; here in the plain its wildness was spent, it was merely broad and yellow. Bergnolte stroked a ginger cat asleep on a stool by the stove, picked up one of the beechwood logs that were stacked beside the stove and smelled it. This was how he was found by the landlord, a portly man of fifty who came into the room tugging briskly at his lapels to adjust the shoulders of his jacket. Bergnolte, startled, decided bravely to hold on to the log, but his sniffing at it was no longer quite so convincing. 'Yes,' said the landlord, who had buttoned his jacket and picked up his cigar again, 'it's genuine all right.' 'Yes, of course,' said Bergnolte, glad to be able to put down the log and get to his table. The landlord followed him with the menu, Bergnolte ordered a glass of beer, got out his notebook and wrote 'Business trip to Birglar: Return ticket (1st class) 6.60.

Taxi station – crthse. 2.30. Phone –' Here he paused, amused and dismayed by the promptings of the despicable fellow inside him to write 1.30 instead of 0.50. While he had been writing the taxi fare this fellow had already been prompting him to write 3.20 instead of 2.30, but at the same time this inner companion had pointed out that the taxi fare would be very easy to check, the distance from station to court-house being more or less constant (that morning, when the taxi-driver, on being asked for a receipt, had offered to write five, six, or eight marks if he wanted, Bergnolte had blushed and asked for the correct amount, including the tip, which he calculated at ten pfennigs); the telephone charge, whispered that invisible companion of his soul, could not possibly be checked, as one could hardly assume that Fräulein Kunrat, Grellber's secretary, would have checked the length of the conversation with a stop watch. Shaking his head, as chagrined by human weakness as he was amused by it, he wrote down the true amount, DM 0.50, then entered the headings 'lunch', 'tips' and 'miscellaneous'. His study of the menu ended, as he had known it would, in favour of that incorrigible gay dog who was likewise concealed within him, that second companion of his soul whose appearance he always greeted with delight. Since, moreover, the most expensive table d'hôte meal – there were four of them, ranging from DM 4.60 (sauerbraten) to 8.50 (veal cutlets with asparagus, pineapple, and fried potatoes) – included one of his favourite desserts, chocolate parfait with whipped cream, he yielded with a sigh to the promptings of the gay dog. He pricked up his ears when he heard the names 'Hännchen' and 'Georg' spoken behind the counter by a young woman whose big, soft grey eyes struck him as being as remarkable as the slim hands with which she affectionately stroked a large, four-tiered food carrier that could also have served as a pie rack. The landlord, not precisely ill-tempered, not even annoyed, but in a voice with a slight touch of irritation, was saying to the young woman in a hybrid German mingled with the thick regional dialect: 'How often do I have to tell you that Hännchen doesn't take milk in his coffee – only Georg does, but all you ever think of is Georg.' He was evidently referring to the contents of an attractive red and black Thermos flask, which he peered into and briefly sniffed before screwing on the cover. 'There,' he said, reaching under the counter and bringing out a slender, expensive-looking cigar from an invisible box apparently kept for his private use, since an ample selection of other cigars was displayed in the glass showcase. 'Give that to Hännchen,' he said. He carefully wrapped the cigar in a paper napkin, slipped it into a metal tube and the tube into the girl's coat pocket, saying: 'But be sure and bring back the tube.'

Bergnolte found himself looking round at the décor of the dining-room, realizing for the first time how handsome it was. The centre pieces of the wood panelling were exquisitely carved in low relief, their contrasts accentuated by subtle variations in staining. On one surface, representing scarcely a twentieth of the whole wall, one large panel was carved with a harvest scene surrounded by tea, coffee, and cocoa shrubs in various stages of blossom and maturity; another field depicted camomile and peppermint, milfoil and linden blossom; between the panels, tall, slim cherry-wood closets, flat, light brown with a reddish sheen. The landlord brought the beer, set it down in front of Bergnolte, followed his gaze, pursed his lips approvingly, and said: 'Yes, there's many a museum would like to have that.' When Bergnolte asked, 'But surely that's not old, that's recent work – whoever produces anything like that nowadays?' the landlord answered darkly: 'That's right, there's a lot of people wouldn't mind paying for that address.' Then he asked Bergnolte whether he preferred consommé or cream of asparagus; Bergnolte chose consommé and, taking a deep draught of beer, wondered whether his question had been too clumsy. (Later in the kitchen the landlord told his wife, who was still speechless from her daughter's sudden announcement that she had 'given herself' to young Gruhl and 'conceived from him'; 'They can't fool me, those court-house characters, I can smell them a mile away.')

In the witness-room the atmosphere during the first hour had been fairly tense; despite their superior officer's violent headshakings, the sergeant and the private first class from the Bundeswehr had immediately approached Frau Seiffert, seen to it that she had a chair, and started up a conversation with her on the latest dances; when it appeared that Frau Seiffert was not a very keen dancer, the sergeant, abetted by the private, switched to the subject of drinks; the private said his favourite was Bloody Mary with a dash of vodka. Frau Seiffert, short-tempered and suffering from lack of sleep due to the early hour, had difficulty in conveying to the sergeant, in a low but increasingly insistent voice, that she hated men who bothered or pawed her so early in the morning, that she didn't like being pestered anyway, and when the sergeant whispered that he found that hard to believe, she said, in a voice no longer so low: 'The baker doesn't always like hot rolls, even when he gets them for nothing,' which the sergeant didn't understand, although the private did, sensing, with some complacency, that he was in Frau Seiffert's good books – although only relatively, for she was irritable with him too. He adopted a becoming air of sophistication and talked about Gin Fizzes and Manhattans, while the sergeant, with rugged virility, expressed his preference for beer and schnapps, thus earning the contempt of Frau Seiffert, who murmured that the only true love-potion was wine. The private was a short, slight fellow with glasses but a powerful mouth and a nose full of character; the sergeant, short-nosed and weak-chinned, tried in vain to signal to him with his eyes to leave Frau Seiffert to him, but with a barely perceptible shake of the head and a contemptuous twist to his lips the private refused. The officer, the superior of both, a young man of somewhat bleakly handsome appearance, was obviously embarrassed by this Bundeswehr-Seiffert alliance; when he heard the word 'vodka' he became very angry. He had long been annoyed by the fact that vodka appeared to be becoming the fashionable drink; he felt – as he had already stated in a letter to the television advertising department – that this vodka craze and vodka advertising harboured insidious softening toward the Russians, a suspicion he found confirmed in the recent popularity of fur hats.

Old Father Kolb of Huskirchen was chatting in an undertone

with two of his parishioners, the younger being Frau Wermelskirchen, a widow, the older being Gruhl's mother-in-law, Frau
Leuffen, née Leuffen, also a widow; the three were quietly discussing a subject that was of very little interest to anyone else
present: which dog had been barking the night before in Huskirchen. Frau Wermelskirchen thought it could only have been
Bello, the German shepherd belonging to Grabel the innkeeper;
Frau Leuffen figured it must have been Berghausen's poodle
Nora, while the priest clung obstinately to the theory that it had
been Pitt, the collie belonging to Leuffen the wheelwright. He
gently pointed out that at his age he spent many a sleepless
night and could recognize all the Huskirchen dogs by their bark,
and Pitt, the wheelwright's collie, was a particularly sensitive,
very intelligent, keen animal that started up at the slightest
sound; he would even begin to bark when the priest sometimes
opened his window in the middle of the night to let out the pipe
smoke, whereas Grabel's German shepherd Bello didn't even
wake up when, as often happened, he went for a walk through
'his sleeping village', from the parsonage to the linden tree and
back and forth again, to get a breath of fresh air; as for Berghausen's poodle, he was simply too timid to bark even if he
woke up. What he liked best of all were the sounds of cows in
the night: their breathing, their coughing, their yawning, and
even those noises which in humans were considered improper
sounded soothing when cows made them, whereas chickens –
chickens were only bearable because they laid eggs. It was also
very pleasant to come upon sleeping birds at night; behind
Grabel's barn – Grabel the farmer, not Grabel the innkeeper –
they often roosted in the apple trees, especially pigeons, although he didn't care for those so much. Frau Wermelskirchen,
the younger of the two women, a sturdy person with black eyes,
said she had never realized the priest went for walks at night,
had Frau Leuffen known about it? Frau Leuffen said, no, she
hadn't; people knew very little about each other, and that was a
pity, people should know more about each other, the good
things too, not only the bad things, whereupon young Frau
Wermelskirchen blushed. Although she was well liked in the

village, her reputation was none too good; she interpreted these remarks of Frau Leuffen's in a way they had not been meant: as an allusion to herself. The priest said he knew many good things about people, although he went for walks in the village at all hours of the night, even at times when usually the less good things were happening; Frau Wermelskirchen blushed still more: the thought that the priest – in his black clothes like a black cat without a cat's plainly visible eyes – might lie in wait or have lain in wait in the village at night, seemed to cause her a good deal of discomfiture, but even the priest's remark had in no way been meant as an allusion to herself. Frau Wermelskirchen said that, since a priest heard almost nothing but bad things in the confessional, she was amazed he thought so well of people; the priest said he thought neither well nor ill of people and that there were some exaggerated ideas about the bad things a priest heard in the confessional, 'but to walk through the village at night when everything's quiet, only the animals a bit restless', well, that was something he just loved, and it made him pity people, no matter how good or bad they might be. In order to reassure Frau Wermelskirchen, who was still red about her ears and bright cheeks, he placed a hand on her arm, saying he didn't mean to be obstinate but the fact was that it had been Leuffen's collie; Frau Wermelskirchen conceded that this might be possible. Ignoring the instructions to priests to abstain from smoking in public, he drew his pipe out of his coat pocket, filled it deliberately from a green, rather scruffy tin on which the words 'Chocolate Mints' were still visible, drew on the cold, full pipe, and gave a start when the young officer – who welcomed the opportunity of getting into conversation with one of the groups – was on the spot rather too quickly with a burning match which, like all non-smokers, he held too close to the priest's nose. The latter, startled and a little put out at the young man's eagerness and the dangerous proximity of the match, glanced nervously round and blew out the match, looking apologetically at the young officer as he did so and saying: 'I'm sorry, I believe we agreed before you came that we wouldn't smoke.' There was an immediate murmur of friendly protest in which Frau Seiffert joined with particular vigour, as did Horn, who was still there; a murmur from which it was clearly audible that he, the priest – first because he was the priest and second because he was by far the most senior person in the room – was to be regarded as an exception. The priest allowed himself to be persuaded on condition that they take turns smoking according to age, and he nodded his thanks when the lieutenant, relieved at not being rejected this time, lit a second match. Repressed, and with the abrupt familiarity common to the repressed, the lieutenant, whom the priest had drawn into the Huskirchen circle with an inimitable gesture of his pipe, now began in a surprisingly harsh voice to discuss the term 'vernacular', which, he said, he had been astonished to find in the most recent reports of the Church Council. Might that not lead to a vulgarization of sacred language? The two women, who were still politely listening, looked expectantly at their priest: they were proud of his cleverness, even when they did not always understand or appreciate it. The priest asked the officer whether he had ever heard the expression 'vulgate'? He had? Well then, he would know that it meant ordinary, or general, in fact 'vulgar' in the sense of what was in common usage among the rank and file; the priest personally felt that the vernacular could not be vulgar enough, and he had already begun to translate the best-known of the Sunday collects into the Huskirchen dialect, which differed considerably from that of Kireskirchen. The two women exchanged proud glances. They were proud of the triumph of their priest's cleverness. The officer did not seem to care for the priest's interpretation; he said he had been thinking more of a strictly exclusive and liturgical German, a German of the élite, in fact – he was not afraid to use the word. The women began to lose interest at this point, even their politeness flagged; they put their heads together behind the priest's back, while he leaned forward to make it easier for them, and discussed their gardens. Frau Leuffen asked Frau Wermelskirchen, who was known to be an expert gardener, whether the dahlias should be taken up now or later; it was too soon to take them out, she said, and there was still time till shortly before the first frost. That was something she never got right, said Frau Leuffen, although she had been looking after her garden for fifty years. How did she manage, year after year, to keep her roses so long in bloom, Frau Leuffen wanted to know, to which Frau Wermelskirchen replied she didn't know herself, really she didn't, she didn't do anything special to them, a remark which Frau Leuffen dismissed with an arch smile and a wink as being 'too modest'. It was a secret, she said, but she quite understood that Frau Wermelskirchen didn't want to give away the secret, and she didn't know herself whether, if she had a secret like that, she would give it away; she had never had a green thumb herself. The two men had now advanced to the topic of religion and theology, which the priest had described as being two completely different fields, thereby calling forth a protest from the officer. It was at this moment that Frau Seiffert was summoned to the witness-stand with the call: 'Come along, Sanni dear, your hour has struck.' The sergeant, whose virile swagger had given Frau Seiffert, as she put it, 'a pain in the neck', now growled openly at the private; the latter strolled nonchalantly – insofar as this can be done in three steps – across to the third group, consisting of Dr Grähn the auditor, Hall the bailiff, Kirffel the income tax inspector (son of the police officer), Horn (at that time still waiting to be called), and Erbel the travelling salesman. These five, all obviously talking about Gruhl, happened to be discussing a subject described by Grähn, the speaker of the moment, as 'structural changes in the manual trades'. The priest announced that, 'in view of his long abstinence', he had finished his pipe 'with unpardonable haste', and that now it was really Horn's turn, but Horn had given up smoking, so, to judge by his limited knowledge of their ages, Hall was next in line, Frau Leuffen – next in age after Horn – also being a non-smoker. Hall happily accepted his lot and put a cigarette between his lips. The two women got up, stood whispering at the door with the sheriff's officer, and disappeared giggling into the far end of the corridor, an area still familiar to the older witnesses – Hall, Kirffel, and Horn – from their schooldays. The three men quickly switched to a new topic, thereby temporarily excluding Grähn and Erbel who were young and new to the place, until they passed beyond school reminiscences and returned to a subject in which Grähn could join: the economic crisis of the twenties.

It was not long before Erbel and Horn were called, whereupon the private, who had realized Grähn was an authority on the subject, asked whether the credit situation among small and medium-sized businesses was as unstable in Birglar County as in his own part of the country; he was from the Bergisch area, where his father worked in the bank. Grähn welcomed the subject, while Hall and Kirffel, once Horn had been called, would have preferred to discuss with Grähn the 'tenor' of their testimony concerning Gruhl. The private was now speaking as casually of such things as fluctuation factors and revolving credit as he had just been discussing Bloody Marys and Manhattans with Frau Seiffert, and they regarded him with undisguised dislike; they moved aside from the two men, forming a group of their own at the window and agreeing in whispers 'not to drag either Johann or Birglar through the dirt'.

When Erbel and Horn were called, shortly after Frau Seiffert, a sigh of relief went through the various groups, especially from the sergeant, whose superior officer had been indicating by insistent nods and glances that he should move over to the window. He greatly disliked the moralistic notions of the lieutenant, who was known in the garrison as Robert the Pious. But when it became clear that the interrogation of Horn was going to take some time and Sterck was asked whether the order of witnesses could be ascertained so that they could take it in turns to go for a cup of coffee, Sterck turned this down, explaining that the object of not announcing the order was to prevent collusion. Then Grähn, who had earned a reputation as an entertainer in the 'Association of Academic Economists', suggested some guessing or forfeit games; he was even prepared, he said with a grin – and begging the pardon of all those present who did not have a religious background – to submit to an hour's quizzing on the catechism by the priest, whereupon the priest said he had never been able to remember the catechism, had never been able to 'get it into his head'. Old Frau Leuffen said she thought this game was 'going too far'; the lieutenant backed her up with a vigorous nod. After this brief, quasi-anarchistic interruption, the witnesses formed new groups: the sergeant, the private, and the bailiff began a game of Skat on the wooden window-seat; Grähn looked on; the lieutenant, who disapproved of cards on principle but did not want to pull rank at a time like this and certainly not in public, went back to the priest, who wished to discuss the state of his parish finances with Kirffel, the honorary treasurer of his parish. He was especially concerned over the misuse of funds with which he had been reproached, funds that had been collected for a bell out of which the greater part had been used to help finance the move of a certain Fiene Schurz, who six years ago had gone to live in the city where she had married that fellow Schurz who had deserted her after begetting their fourth child; this Fiene Schurz, née Kirffel, had thereupon succumbed to an unsuspected lack of moral fibre that had only come to light when, in order to preserve her children from destitution, she had taken a job as a waitress in a bar; in short: she had had to be brought back to her parents' home in Huskirchen because she had been induced by her employer, an irresponsible fellow by the name of Keller, 'to do a bit of stripping' in the bar where she worked as a waitress. The priest, in this discussion of confidential matters, felt that perhaps the lieutenant's joining them did not exactly show 'a want of tact', but nevertheless, as he later declared, 'that boy has a strange way of butting in'. Well, anyway: the priest had misused the bell funds to make it possible for Fiene Schurz to move back to her native Huskirchen (in vain, as he was now beginning to realize but was not yet ready to admit, for Frau Schurz, knowing her children to be in her mother's care, took the train every evening to the city, 'no longer', as it turned out, 'only to strip'). At this point, the premature intervention of the lieutenant caused a slight, almost ludicrous misunderstanding for which Kirffel was not entirely blameless either. The lieutenant who, as he said himself, was a 'keen signals man', knew the expression 'strip' only as a

variation of stripping cables, a term familiar to every soldier in
the signals branch; the innocent Kirffel II also knew the word
in this and only this sense, and both men, Kirffel and the lieutenant, were persuaded for a time that Fiene Schurz had a job
stripping cables at night for a private telephone company: a
strange idea, especially as they could not understand why the
work had to be done at night. The lieutenant at once became
suspicious that this might involve intelligence work for a 'foreign power'; Kirffel's head was buzzing anyway, mainly because
he would soon have to testify in the Gruhl case, but also because, by misusing the funds, the priest had got himself involved in difficulties transcending anything he himself could yet
envisage; finally the old priest, who could not understand why
the two men were going on about telephones, became impatient
and said: 'But gentlemen, she isn't a call girl, she's just a strip-
per.' He added, with that sardonic humour that made him the
favourite guest at every parsonage: 'I wouldn't put it past her
to do both in the long run: to strip *and* be a call girl.' Kirffel II
and the lieutenant stared at the priest, completely bewildered; a
kind of mutual liking began to make itself felt between the two
men, since it struck both of them as definitely odd to hear the
word 'call girl' uttered so casually by a priest and neither of
them had yet quite grasped the ulterior meaning of 'stripping'
in what was evidently an immoral context. The lieutenant must
see now, said the priest, whose voice had lost all its jocularity.
how important it was to be familiar with the vernacular; moreover, he had meanwhile found out that Fiene Schurz, with
whose moral future he was greatly concerned, was carrying on
this objectionable occupation in the city in a bar 'swarming with
Bundeswehr officers and members of the legislature from the
Christian Democrat and Christian Socialist parties' who had
the nerve 'to set themselves up as watchdogs of Christian morality'. The lieutenant replied rather sharply that it was wrong to
generalize from such 'isolated observations'. The majority of
Bundeswehr officers were men of irreproachable character who
insisted on moral purity, unfortunately – he remarked with a
glance at the chair on which Frau Seiffert had been sitting and

which was now occupied by Frau Wermelskirchen – unfortunately not always with success, morality not yet being one of those items which could be regulated by orders. The priest looked at him gravely and said: 'It is from wood like yours that the best Communists are carved,' a remark that caused the lieutenant not, as might have been expected, to protest, but to ponder.

Frau Wermelskirchen and Frau Leuffen, in quieter whispers than the three men, were also discussing the Schurz affair, and surprisingly enough young Frau Wermelskirchen was far more severe in her judgement of Fiene Schurz than the older woman was. The latter laid most of the blame on the absconding husband, whereas Frau Wermelskirchen, while admitting herself to be a 'sensual and somewhat irresponsible person', regarded 'doing that kind of thing for money' as the truly outrageous feature of Fiene Schurz's depravity. Frau Leuffen disagreed, saying that women who 'did that kind of thing for money' were actually less of a threat because they 'merely performed a service for men', while women who didn't take money were worse because they 'got the men involved'; Frau Wermelskirchen, who always took everything personally, said she had never got any man involved – she had always left them their freedom. However, at this point, when the tension in all three groups was almost at the point of explosion – even among the Skat players, where the private had had a streak of good luck and the sergeant nothing but bad cards – at this point the sheriff's officer flung open the door and announced the hour-and-a-half noon recess.

Before going home for lunch, Stollfuss asked the attorneys for the prosecution and the defence to join him in the upper floor of the building, where he invited them to a brief stand-up procedural conference in the corridor concerning the remaining nine witnesses. He was wondering whether there was any hope of speeding up proceedings and hearing all nine that afternoon if the witnesses were interrogated somewhat more rapidly and irrelevant questions were avoided, or whether it would be advisable to dismiss some of them for the afternoon – old Father Kolb, for instance, and Frau Leuffen, who was almost as old as he was – and tell them to come back the next day. After deliberating for a few moments, the defence attorney said that, as far as he was concerned, he could restrict the interrogation of the private, the sergeant, old Frau Leuffen, and the priest to ten minutes each; but when it came to the lieutenant, whose evidence went to the very heart of the matter, well, for him he would probably need half an hour, while again Grähn and Kirffel II could no doubt be dealt with in twenty minutes each, since they were testifying almost exclusively in their capacity as experts. So, if it were up to him, the hearing could be completed today, with the pleadings taking place perhaps tomorrow – although he must admit he couldn't foresee how much time would be required for Frau Wermelskirchen, who had been called by his colleague. The district attorney, not nearly as aggressive and intransigent as he had sometimes appeared in the courtroom, in fact quite jovial, said he would need Frau Wermelskirchen for ten minutes at the most and couldn't his distinguished colleague cut short his interrogation of the lieutenant, seeing that his inclusion as a witness implied what was actually a superfluous emphasis of the political aspect, since the case could really be considered closed, whereupon the defence attorney said it was not he but his distinguished colleague who was introducing a political element into the case, 'the actual intellectual content of which scarcely went beyond the mentality of smugglers and poachers', which reminded him that he had called an additional witness for the afternoon, an art dealer by the name of Motrik from the city. Moreover, Professor Büren, of the Fine Arts Department, had also been called as a witness for the late afternoon. 'Very well then,' said the judge impatiently, 'let's not send anyone home, but, if you don't mind, let's show some consideration toward the older ones by taking them first.' The two younger lawyers helped him on with his coat, which had been hanging in the corridor on the old-fashioned hook where high school students had once hung their caps – each attorney held one shoulder to assist the old gentleman, and the defence attorney hung the judge's robe on the empty hook.

*

Witnesses and spectators now distributed themselves according to social status among the various restaurants of Birglar. While the men were having their brief colloquy upstairs, Frau Hermes introduced herself to Frau Kugl-Egger and suggested they should go ahead to the Duhr Terraces; Frau Kugl-Egger, a shy person, had been born in Birglar; not only had she approved her husband's desire to be transferred here, she had actively encouraged it for the sake of a wealthy old uncle called Schorf who wanted to have her, 'his pet', close at hand. Frau Hermes knew the background to the Kugl-Egger transfer, and she also appreciated the diffidence with which 'Grabel's Marlies' – as Frau Kugl-Egger had been known before her marriage – first began to circulate on her native soil; she even spoke Bavarian dialect, and in a soft voice talked about the small provincial town in Bavaria, far away down there beyond the forests, which Frau Hermes always referred to as 'that little place east of Nuremberg'. With determined affability Frau Hermes took Frau Kugl-Egger by storm, so to speak; after fifty paces she linked arms with her, and after sixty paces ascertained that Frau Kugl-Egger was also a Catholic (she had a vague idea there were some Protestant areas in Bavaria!), and began with typical Rhineland volubility to talk about her plans for the Catholic Academic Society's St Nicholas ball, which, she said, she was determined to 'invade then and there with some modern touches', especially with regard to the dances normally considered acceptable there. She was also planning a 'frank discussion of sexual problems, including the Pill'. Before they had quite covered the scant five minutes' walk to the Duhr Terraces, she already knew the size in square feet of the Kugl-Eggers' new Huskirchen apartment, that they had, 'needless to say', been taken for a ride by the highest-priced decorator in the area, and that their rent was excessive, but – and this seemed to make up for the rest – they had landed in the parish of the nicest priest anywhere in the whole district; and of course – this topic came up immediately when Frau Kugl-Egger happened to say what a hard time her children were going to have with their Bavarian accent – of course one could argue for hours, days even, about the blessings or otherwise of nuns in kindergartens. Frau Kugl-Egger, the shorter of the two and the younger by a few years, felt, as she confided to her husband afterward, 'on the one hand caught off guard and on the other fascinated by the speed' with which she was swept into the Catholic academic life of Birglar. They had now reached the restaurant and seen Bergnolte who, handling his spoon in an unexpectedly old-world manner, was in the act of consuming his chocolate parfait – anyway, said Frau Hermes, 'a lot of stuffiness had still to be got rid of in Birglar' and the fresh air of freedom needed to blow through 'certain Catholic marriages'.

Frau Kugl-Egger was somewhat relieved when Frau Hermes ordered two Cinzanos with ice; she had been afraid she would order something stronger, although at the same time she realized the odd contrast between Frau Hermes' alarming tempo and the frank, round, fair-complexioned face which she found herself searching in vain for signs of malice. She was also relieved to note that the Cinzanos were not a prelude to endearments; Frau Hermes merely raised her glass and welcomed her with a 'To your happy homecoming, Marlies!' Frau Kugl-Egger, while she studied the menu without really reading it, was wondering whether Frau Hermes might have been that temperamental blonde with a dubious reputation who had been two grades ahead of her in school at Birglar: a lively, fat, blonde girl, always laughing, whom she remembered as 'somehow forever chewing an apple'. Her father – whatever was his name? – had carried on a brisk and not always entirely legal business in fertilizers, coal, and seed. Oh well, she would find all that out in a quarter of an hour at most.

Before very long, a group entered which Frau Hermes, in a voice not all that inaudible, described as 'liberal advanced': Dr Grähn, Frau Schorf-Kreidel, and Aussem; a brief wave from Frau Schorf-Kreidel and a suggestion of a bow from both Grähn and Aussem, who sat down at the table next to Bergnolte, evidently desirous of the view of the muddy waters of the Duhr, described by Frau Hermes not as a river but as sluggish porridge.

Kugl-Egger and Hermes now entered the restaurant together, roaring with laughter at a joke one had just told, and Hermes introduced himself to Frau Kugl-Egger as 'one of her cousins, although somewhat remote'; they were related, he said, through his maternal grandmother via the Halls from Ober-Birglar: she had been an aunt of Frau Kugl-Egger's uncle Schorf, through whom, incidentally, she was also related to the lady sitting over there, whom she would or could soon embrace as her 'dear cousin Margot' – as Hermes expressed it with a faintly malicious grin – depending, he said, how one got along with this fashionable personage: her only complaint was boredom, and the guilty conscience issuing from this boredom usually prompted her to make false or ungracious statements. Hermes' torrent of speech, scarcely inferior to his wife's, seemed 'almost French' to Frau Kugl-Egger. Although, said Hermes, he didn't care in the least, not the least bit, for local specialities, he could recommend the sauerbraten; everything served here was excellent; Frau Schmitz, the proprietor's wife, was even adept at simple things like potato pancakes and, indeed, even turned the most ordinary stew into a delicacy. (It so happened that Hermes erred in this prediction; on that particular day, for the first but not the only time, Frau Schmitz did everything wrong, so deeply had the announcement of her daughter Eva – that she had given herself to young Gruhl and conceived from him – affected her in her nature, her mentality, her very existence, the worst shock being the knowledge that her first grandchild had been conceived in prison. With Frau Kugl-Egger, this faulty prediction earned Hermes the irrevocable and irreparable reputation of a false prophet or – which Hermes found even more embarrassing – of a poor connoisseur of the culinary art.) It was here that Frau Kugl-Egger managed for the first time to interrupt the genial flow of Hermes' speech by inserting the remark that it wasn't that easy to make a good tasty stew, and as for potato pancakes, they really were tricky; she had tried – out of nostalgia for her native specialities – to make them in that 'little place east of Nuremberg', but without success. She would so much like to know, she went on, availing herself of the breach, whether

Hermes was really as involved in this strange Gruhl business as he seemed; she was the wife of a civil servant who was far from wanting to stick his neck out, however.... But Hermes had leaped into the breach again and was telling her some of his family traditions: how his ancestor Hermes had helped plant the freedom tree in Birglar and had had no love for Napoleon but still less for the Prussians who had brought with them nothing but gendarmes, laws, and taxes.

Meanwhile Frau Hermes had turned to Kugl-Egger – 'I can't resist it' – and mentioned his fiasco with Frau Seiffert, predicting that the same thing would happen with Frau Wermelskirchen; Kugl-Egger laughed, admitting his defeat as far as Frau Seiffert was concerned, and added that what surprised him was not that Frau Seiffert chose to live in a little place like Birglar but that she could make a living there, considering the much greater and more anonymous opportunity offered by the city for followers of her profession. Frau Hermes said surely he must be familiar from legal history with the 'guillotine boundary'; it coincided with the 'bordello boundary', which in turn was also a denominational boundary, and the guillotine boundary – i.e., the boundary of the Napoleonic Code – was even younger than the much older 'sex boundary', the technical craft of which was more strongly emphasized on this, the Catholic side of the border, than the emotional and barbaric aspects on the other side. But what seemed more important to her at the moment – and he could, if he chose, interpret this as an attempt to influence him in favour of her husband's clients, but it wasn't – he had better avoid a similar fiasco with Frau Wermelskirchen; certainly his questions should be confined to the facts and not Gruhl's character. When Kugl-Egger asked if Frau Wermelskirchen 'was also one of those', Frau Hermes said no, she wasn't 'one of those'; she wasn't a prostitute, she was a sinner, 'the kind that three hundred years ago would have been burned as a witch'. There really was something mysterious about Frau Wermelskirchen; the flowers in her garden were often in full bloom long past their normal time, and although she considered herself completely modern in outlook, she felt there was something inexplicable about Frau Wermelskirchen, something like a manifestation of the ancient Celtic cult of matriarchy. But she wasn't even pretty, said Kugl-Egger, whereupon Frau Hermes laughed and said that nowadays nine out of ten women and girls were pretty – that wasn't the point, the district attorney should take a look at Frau Wermelskirchen's eyes and hands, then he would know what a goddess looked like; no, no, she said, as she attacked her cream of asparagus soup with a good appetite, he'd better steer clear of Frau Wermelskirchen; of course she had had an affair with Gruhl senior, but what was he going to gain by bringing that up?

Frau Schorf-Kreidel, who found young Aussem's preoccupation with her minute neck wound rather tiresome, 'almost erotic', as she said later on (he got up several times, stood in front of her, and shook his head as he examined the tiny red blister which she no longer even felt) – Frau Schorf-Kreidel switched the conversation to the Gruhl case, which she described as 'weird'. Yes, agreed Aussem, weirdly absurd; for such cases – where the accused pleaded guilty and did not insist on a trial – he would introduce summary courts; after all, the offence was not strictly speaking a criminal one, it was more anti-social, something that he personally regarded as much more dangerous than a 'clear-cut criminal case'. Grähn said that, while he couldn't of course anticipate his testimony, 'that fellow Gruhl' – well, he was inclined to admire him; there was a tremendous intelligence hidden there. He couldn't understand, said Aussem, why at least Hollweg had not sent a reporter to cover this strange trial, which looked to him like nothing more than a nice farewell party for the venerable Stollfuss and the equally venerable Kirffel. 'All it really amounts to is an office party,' he said, jumping to his feet again to have another look, accompanied by much tongue-clucking, at the tiny red mark, the size of a matchhead, on Frau Schorf-Kreidel's neck, and adding that this would be an eternal reminder to her and all her admirers of the Gruhl trial.

The entry of some of the staff from the local civic administration building, who came in shifts for their lunch at the Duhr Terraces, caused a slight disturbance and voices had to be lowered. Over his cup of coffee Bergnolte wondered whether a 'tip', in terms of an expense account, was to be regarded subjectively or objectively; objectively of course, he thought, and he had to admit his manifest unfamiliarity with the relevant regulations. From a purely abstract point of view, he was interested to know whether the state could approve 'generosity' in tipping; probably, he thought with a sigh, it was a matter of rank, and obviously a judge could leave a bigger tip than a counsellor : it was little things like this that revealed the remnants of the old concept of grace and favour, which existed only within the framework of power; in popular terms : the more powerful a man was, the more grace and favour, the more largesse, he could dispense.

Sergeant Behlau had been making vain attempts to get into Frau Seiffert's bar, which he discovered in a side street; it was called the Red Lantern. He spent some time thumping on the door and jamming his finger on the bell until finally a window on the first floor opened to reveal a coarse-looking individual exposing a broad expanse of black chest-hair, who threatened, if Behlau didn't clear out immediately, to sue him for breach of the peace; it was obvious from the fellow's voice that he was a foreigner, probably an American; also clearly audible in the background was Frau Seiffert's voice, talking about 'that cheapskate soldier on the make'. Behlau conceded his defeat and returned to a less disreputable place – cheaper, too, incidentally – where he had seen Private Kuttke going in. It was called the Jug of Beer; regular dinners were not served there, but there were hearty, satisfying short orders : good thick soup, potato salad, wieners, bouillon, and meat-balls; a place for truck drivers and workmen, with jukeboxes and pinball games for entertainment that one would have looked for in vain at the Duhr Terraces.

Behlau found the private deep in conversation at the counter with two truck drivers whom he was impressing, but at the same time rendering somewhat suspicious, with his fund of knowledge about types of automobiles, braking distances, lubrication, axle loads, and inspection periods; the various defeats suffered by the sergeant during the morning had left him with no taste for the company of the private at lunch-time as well, so he sat down on a bar stool in the opposite corner, ordered sausage on rye with onions and – this surprised him as much as it did the landlord, who had seen at once that he was a beer-drinker – a carafe of wine; his neighbour at the bar, a melancholy, introspective-looking middle-aged travelling salesman who sat there listlessly turning his beer glass with one hand and wistfully stroking his bald head with the other, asked him whether things in the army were the same as they had been in his day; the sergeant promptly replied: 'Probably just the same,' and then embarked on his favourite topic: the difference in pay among NATO troops. It caused bad blood, he said, especially when it came to women; things had now got to the point where whenever you arrived some place there was always an American in bed ahead of you, but thank God most of those were married and moral, and those poor bastards, the Belgians and the French, were far worse off even than the Germans; no, he said when the salesman asked how the Dutch and the Danes were paid, no, said Behlau, he had no idea, all he knew was that the Italians were the worst off of the lot, but – as far as he knew – they weren't always being confronted with those dollar-happy Americans, like the Germans and those poor Belgians and French.

Father Kolb had considered inviting himself for dinner and a good cup of coffee at his Birglar colleague's; his answer to this question was a theoretical Yes, but then he decided not to pursue this theoretical idea; the newly appointed local priest, whom he had met only once at a deanery conference and whom he had rather liked, had been chosen – as had been hinted to him 'in the city' – to examine his, Kolb's, discrepancies in the bell-funds affair, and a visit to him might easily be interpreted as a request for leniency and lead to humiliating results. So he joined his two lady parishioners who were making for a place known only to the locals, one might almost say only to the initiated: Frohn's Bakery, in whose back room, which was actually the Frohns' living-room turned into an improvised café, good coffee and very good cakes were served, and, if desired, an excellent home-made soup to which could be added a thick slice of bacon or chopped sausage. Kolb was also attracted by the chance of a heart-to-heart talk with Frau Wermelskirchen under conditions less public than the witness-room; he was determined to set her mind at rest that neither he nor anyone else in the village was spying on her during those nocturnal walks. Blaming himself for making such an elementary mistake, he was already regretting his rashness in telling the women about those walks; as a matter of fact, he didn't go for these walks nearly so often as would now become common gossip: perhaps once or twice, at most three times, a month, when his insomnia got the better of him and he had had his fill of reading and prayer. True, he had once seen a man coming out of Frau Wermelskirchen's house about three or four in the morning, and had even recognized him; but he wouldn't even *think* his name, much less identify him, and even when he met him – he often ran across him – he did not think *every* time of his secret nocturnal escapade.

Frohn's Bakery was located at some distance from Birglar's modernized main street, in a part of town that still retained its village-like atmosphere. Kolb – no prophecy was needed to foretell this – assumed that Frau Leuffen would be invited to join the Frohns in the kitchen at the family table; Frau Wermelskirchen, with her reputation, would not be accorded this honour, while he, the priest, because it would have been too insignificant an honour for him, would not be offered the kitchen. His assumption turned out to be partially correct: Frau Leuffen was immediately conducted into the kitchen; he entered the café with Frau Wermelskirchen but found two other guests there: Herr and Frau Scholwen, from Kireskirchen, who had been to see the notary about buying a piece of land and now immediately got into conversation with Frau Wermelskirchen; the latter was known to be a shrewd real estate saleswoman, for she made a living selling her inherited property piece by piece and buying land at the right time; here, too, she was credited with a 'sixth sense'. The priest accepted the invitation to join the other three at the large table, which was adorned with a plush table-cloth; an open tureen containing the last of the vegetable soup reminded him of his appetite. In unadulterated dialect the Scholwens exchanged opinions with Frau Wermelskirchen about land prices in Kireskirchen, where the Scholwens had given up farming and built themselves a bungalow. Frau Schol-wen's capacious black purse, lying open on the table, seemed to indicate that they were just about to leave.

Lieutenant Heimüller had glanced briefly into the Jug of Beer but was not in the mood for exchanging beery confidences with his two subordinates or submitting to veiled, quasi-intellectual insults such as he fully believed Private Kuttke capable of. He walked slowly along the main street of Birglar, rejected the two largish modern cafés which were crammed with apprentices and vocational, agricultural, and high school students, and, after hesitating too long, ended up in the Duhr Terraces where he found such lively chattering going on at all the tables that he felt not only miserable but like a fish out of water, an outsider, and was relieved to discover an unoccupied table. The spirited conversation, mingled with much laughter, at the next table where Frau Hermes and Frau Kugl-Egger were trying to con-sole themselves for the disastrous meal by making a joke of it; the quiet but intensely confidential discussion going on between Frau Schorf-Kreidel, Dr Grähn, and Aussem; even Bergnolte's pose of sophisticated enjoyment – he was indulging in a cigar (having waited in vain for the landlord to produce one from under the counter) – the whole atmosphere seemed hostile to him, although not a single person present was harbouring an evil thought. Even the clerks from the administration building, daily regulars who at that moment got up and stood laughing and chatting with two or three girls, obviously secretaries, seemed to him to be showing their contempt. He stood up, went over to the rack, and got himself one of the national news-papers.

Among those who went home for lunch was Horn, whose

wife served him bacon pancakes, salad, and lemon cream. After lunch, over a cup of coffee, he discussed with her the problem of 'co-education during puberty', a subject that was to be debated at the 'Socialist Study Group for Education' over which Frau Horn, a former schoolteacher, had consented to preside. Horn wisely said nothing about the fines that had been imposed on him. Grete Horn, a slender white-haired woman with very dark eyes, classified all the men – including her husband – connected with the Gruhl case as 'numskulls' who failed to see what opportunities were being missed by not giving publicity to the case. 'Just imagine,' she said calmly, 'what would happen if all the soldiers hit on the idea of setting fire to their jeeps and planes! But those ridiculous Social Democrats, those hypocritical crooks, they're more capitalist now than the capitalists.' Horn, who was used to these and even more cutting remarks from his wife, shook his head and said all he cared about was getting Gruhl out of jail as quickly as possible and with a light sentence. She said Gruhl wasn't worried about a year or two in jail, he would find a job as a carpenter even in the penitentiary, since those 'wardens' wives' were probably just as mad about period furniture as all the other capitalist 'tabbies'; the only thing was, she added, with a smile that gave her hard mouth a sudden charm, the only thing was that of course Gruhl would have to manage without women in jail, but that was all.

The fact that his wife served him his favourite dish – stuffed green peppers – was enough to indicate to Hubert Hall, the bailiff, that once again she was going to ask for leniency for one of his clients: and indeed, when she gave him his dessert, coffee custard with cream, she admitted that a Frau Schöffler had been to see her to ask if she couldn't persuade him to put off impounding her small car; she could take care of the matter in two days, three at the most, and he must realize, Frau Schöffler had said, how hard it was to get back any impounded article 'from the claws of those hyenas'. Hall, who to his wife's surprise remained even-tempered, said there was nothing he could do about it and he would get into the devil of a mess if he tried;

the Schöffler woman had already been guilty of contempt of court several times, having on one occasion taken the tubes out of an impounded radio set and sold them to a junk dealer in the city for the price of a cup of coffee and a slice of cream cake; no, no, he would put it off for one more day, but no longer, she could tell the Schöffler woman that.

Kirffel II, the income tax inspector, as popular in Birglar as his father, the police inspector, found his wife almost in tears, although he was glad to see she was being calmed down by his daughter Birgit and his son Frank, who had also taken pity on the midday meal by rescuing the noodles from burning and saving the sauce, made from corned beef, paprika, and peas, from boiling down to 'a disgusting paste', and had produced some macaroons and coffee for dessert, 'to brighten things up a bit'.

The distress of Frau Kirffel, known to almost everyone as a 'splendid woman', had started when a young artist had delivered his paintings to the Kirffel apartment at about eleven-thirty that morning. After protracted negotiations Kirffel – who, because he found it hard to say no, was chairman of almost every club in Birglar, including the 'Association for the Promotion of Regional Artists' – had obtained permission from the authorities to hold exhibitions in the lobby of the small finance building, and at the last committee meeting (at which Frau Hermes had again shown herself to be a daring, taboo-defying modernist) it had been decided to start with one-man shows rather than multiple exhibitions: for two weeks at a time, an artist chosen by a jury was to have an opportunity of exhibiting his works to such of the taxpayers of Birglar County as were compelled to visit the finance department. After drawing lots, Number One turned out to be Tervel, a distant nephew of the police inspector, who, while proud of his relative, was at the same time repelled by his paintings. Young Tervel had already 'got himself talked about' in the city papers and had even been mentioned briefly in the national press. At first he had wanted to refuse the invitation to exhibit in the Birglar finance building as 'an attempt to pin me down to this provincial dump'; however, the critic Kernehl (art teacher at Birglar High School, young Tervel's former teacher, fatherly friend, and patron) had convinced him that he simply could not refuse: after all, people in Birglar County had eyes like anyone else. In short, Tervel (whose paintings were later described in the *Rhineland Review* as 'genital daubs', in the *Rhineland Daily News* – where Kernehl wrote the art reviews under the pseudonym of Opticus – as 'bold sexual statements', and by Hollweg, who wrote his own art reviews in the Duhr Valley *Courier*, as 'hopeful-hopeless') Tervel had deposited his paintings (six, the number allotted him, of which four measured six by ten feet) at about eleven-thirty at Frau Kirffel's, or rather, carried them with the help of a friend into the Kirffel's none-too-large living-room; there he was enraged to find a painting by his colleague Schorf, whom he consistently referred to as an 'abstract dabbler'. Frau Kirffel was afraid less of the scandal than of the paintings themselves, which scared her, as she admitted to her children on their return from school; hence they found her in the act of spreading a sheet over one painting that she called 'particularly revolting', one of the six-by-ten-foot canvases. In muddy red, purple, and murky brown it depicted the blurred but still recognizable outlines of a naked young man standing beside a naked prone lady, frying eggs over yellowish-blue flames spouting from the gas burners which were her breasts; the picture was entitled 'Breakfast for Two'. Most of the other paintings, in which the muddy red was predominant, showed couples involved in acts of love; it was a cycle entitled 'The Sacrament of Marriage'. Kirffel himself, as soon as he had soothed his wife and consented to covering the paintings with sheets, began to get cold feet as he ate his lunch, his thoughts elsewhere; most of all he was afraid of the (indeed, not unwarranted) wrath of the taxpayers: after all, they did not enter the finance building by choice, and then perforce to be confronted with this art might well make them suspect a misuse of their taxes. No doubt the parents of underage citizens, who often came to the finance department in the morning to have tax deductions entered on their cards, would be indignant. (To his surprise – not disappointment, as his few detractors try to insinuate – there was no scandal whatever; only a teenager, later identified as the grandson of Frohn the baker, stuck a slip of paper to the painting 'Breakfast for Two' with the comment: 'Must have swallowed natural gas – cuts down the gas bill.') Young Tervel was offended at the lack of scandal, since there had been one even in the city. Promising to have the paintings – 'draped, covered right up' – removed that very day to his office where a second jury session wanted to have another look at Tervel's work, Kirffel was able to pacify his wife and finish lunch with his giggling children. When asked how the Gruhl trial was coming along, Kirffel said he had no idea; the witnesses didn't get a chance 'to pick up so much as a scrap'.

In the Schroer kitchen sat Schroer, the sheriff's officer (who also performed the duties of janitor and jail warder), his wife Lisa, Sterck, the sheriff's officer from the city, and Kirffel senior, over a lunch of pork chops, mixed salad, and boiled potatoes, the men in shirt-sleeves with beer bottles beside them. Sterck, who had started to unpack the sandwiches he had brought along and unscrew his Thermos flask, had been told brusquely by Frau Schroer 'not to be so snooty' and to join them at table; she had been expecting him anyway, and in case he felt offended at being invited to dinner she would have no objection to his returning the compliment the next time she paid a visit to the city. Sterck's question as to whether he might send or take his sandwiches and 'excellent coffee' to the two accused men in their cell, since they were having a very trying day, was greeted with mocking laughter. Kirffel, in a good mood since he felt his testimony had done no appreciable harm to either his honour or that of the two Gruhls, advised Sterck to enlist in the Bundeswehr, see that he was sent on an official mission, set fire to the car, get himself locked up, and then, of course, provide himself with a son who was able to turn the head of the prettiest girl in Birglar, whose father was Schmitz the restaurant proprietor and whose mother was the best cook for miles around. Sterck, who was enjoying Frau Schroer's meal but did not understand the allusions, was asked, when the doorbell rang, to open the door and take the young lady who would be standing there to the two prisoners, but first, as regulations demanded, to examine the tray for prohibited objects: then, so it was prophesied, he would understand. Sterck did as he was told. Frau Schroer took advantage of his absence to ask Kirffel senior how things were going now between him and his son: today he had had a golden opportunity to get together with him in the witness-room and bury the hatchet, instead of which he had 'sat gloomily here in the kitchen by the stove waiting to be called'. Sighing, Kirffel wiped his mouth with a large serviette, stared at the chocolate pudding Frau Schroer had already placed on the table, and said ominously that it was a cross he had to bear and would have to keep on bearing; everything in his son's house was so grand that he didn't dare go and see him. 'For a policeman like me,' he said, 'who as a young fellow used to play cards with the tramps he locked up – it's all happened too fast. Besides, my son's betrayed me, hasn't he?' He was alluding to a situation which still grieved him deeply: he had sent his son to high school to become a priest, but, although the boy had matriculated (Kirffel said matircalated) and had even taken two semesters of theology, he had, in Kirffel's opinion, fallen for 'the first dolled-up bit of fluff'; and this was the trouble, this bit of fluff, this Frau Kirffel known to everyone as 'that splendid woman'. 'I'll never forgive him for that.' Schroer and his wife both shook their heads and tried to persuade him over the pudding to be reasonable about it after all these years, but Kirffel said this was neither a question of years nor a matter of reason, or would they say religion was a matter of reason? The Schroers had no answer to this; moreover, at this point Sterck returned and resumed his place without a word; he shook his head while finishing his plate and then, in response to glances from the Schroers and Kirffel, said he thought *this* was going too far. The cigar must have cost at least a mark fifty, and the meal, well, he didn't even care for such fancy things – a severe look from Frau Schroer made him correct himself to 'such expensive things', then, almost stuttering, he took that back too and said he meant such rich people's grub; when he saw from Frau Schroer's expression that that was wrong too, as this degraded her food to proletarian grub, he finished up with: 'Oh hell, you know what I mean; a woman who can cook like you do doesn't have to take offence.' This partially placated Frau Schroer and she served him some dessert and a cup of coffee, of which he said later that it was 'out of this world'.

In her spacious old villa, Agnes Hall occupied herself in various ways; first of all, after returning from court, she sat down in her hat and coat at the piano and played a Beethoven sonata, her fine-featured face no longer expressing either scorn or sullen defiance, but rather a wistful triumph. What she didn't know, had never been told because no one would ever tell her, was that she played very well, and she did something that would have horrified music lovers: she broke off after the second movement, placed a cigarette between her lips and went on playing: precisely, her tone almost too brilliant, by the open windows, hoping the music would penetrate as far as the court-house although she was playing not for him but for that other whom only she knew about and whom all those fools in the world would never know about. She broke off again after the third movement, lit another cigarette, continued playing; he had not been the first, or the second: the third, and she in her early forties (she smiled as she transformed the four of forties with 'early'); wartime, of course, the end, and in a confusion of spirit her thoughts now turned to the trial and that man Gruhl, whom she liked and always had liked: she would give him the money to pay for that jeep. He had done the only sensible thing to do with military vehicles: set it on fire; she closed the piano, laughed, and made up her mind to appear there once more late that afternoon, as a spectator and not to hurt dear old Alois's feelings again; but she would tell Hermes she was going to pay for the jeep, maybe Gruhl's unpaid taxes too, and another jeep, and another, in case he set fire to them all; this seemed to her nothing short of an inspiration.

She took off her hat and coat, not bothering to look in the

mirror: she knew how handsome she still was; in the kitchen she broke two eggs into the frying pan, poured some Madeira over them, a touch – hardly more than a few drops – of vinegar, pepper, and mushrooms, unfortunately out of a can, lit the gas rings, put water on for the coffee, and, while her eggs slowly thickened in the pan, peeled herself an apple: nothing, nothing, nothing would be left but a handful, a little handful of dust – as much as would go into a salt shaker. The slice of bread popped up in the toaster; she took it out with her left hand, stirred the eggs with her right, then with her left hand poured water into the coffee filter, and groped in the drawer for the chocolates: one, two – no, she wanted to stay slim and beautiful for all those fools in the world who obeyed the laws, written and unwritten, sacred and secular. Carrying the eggs, coffee, chocolates, two slices of toast, and the butter in the pretty little bowl, she laughed gaily as she moved over to the music room, where the table was laid; how charming it looked, with the candlestick and the carafe of red wine; she lit the candle, placing beside it the slender little cigar given her by Schmitz, another fool; the only thing he knew about was tobacco, nothing about the one true thing in life, this thing called love. The eggs were excellent, or rather *very nearly* excellent, too much vinegar, one or two drops possibly; the toast was excellent: brown as a leaf, the coffee, the chocolates, the slender cigar from Señor Castro's native land – he was another fool – everything was excellent; even the candle was excellent. After clearing away she turned to the strangest of all her occupations: she changed her will. No, not that silly Maria who had become a non-bleeding girl again long before her time, not that dear old fogy Alois, not even the nun who believed in the Son of Man and loved Him – they were all too old, and they were well taken care of anyway: Gruhl was to become the heir to her fortune, on the *one* condition that once a year he set fire to a car; that wouldn't cost him too much, only half the income. Once a year he could light this little candle in remembrance, hold a fiery sacrament for her, and, if he liked, he could sing that – what was it called now? – that All Saints' Litany: St Agnes, St Cecilia, St Catherine – *ora pro nobis*; she laughed, Kirffel had told her how they had both been singing. In sky-blue ink, the slender Castro cigar between her lips, she wrote slowly: 'I hereby bequeath my whole estate, both real and personal, to *Johann* Heinrich Georg Gruhl, of Huskirchen, Birglar County....' It looked very nice, written in sky-blue ink in her firm, vigorous handwriting on the white sheet of paper: strange, remarkable, how much strength there was in a salt shaker, a matchbox, of dust, how much malice, beauty, and elegance – and how much of this thing called love; every year a burning torch, a fiery sacrament to St Agnes, patron saint of the betrothed!

Deep in thought, his half-smoked cigar cold between his lips, Stollfuss started to walk home, after asking his secretary to let his wife know he was coming; he had walked that way so often – across the little municipal park, past the controversial war memorial, a few hundred yards along the Duhr to the old-fashioned villa built in the nineties and inherited by his wife – so often that usually he did not rouse himself and become aware of his surroundings until he was hanging up his hat and coat in the hall and placing his stick in the umbrella stand; and he did not really come fully to his senses until he called Maria, his wife, who at this hour was usually still upstairs making beds or, as she herself put it, 'messing around' in her desk drawers. She was considered a 'scatterbrain' in Birglar: a poor housewife but a good cook and a passionate knitter, the products of whose nimble, tireless hands were worn by Stollfuss on his hands and feet. He also wore them as sweaters on his chest and had them as cushion covers on his chair in the office, and the baby clinic was always kept supplied with infants' layettes that were distributed by doctors and social workers to young mothers; the neediness of these young mothers was something Frau Stollfuss left to the decision of those in charge, but she also urged them to give away little jackets and pants to unneedy mothers. It was always said of her, Maria Stollfuss née Hollweg, that she was never in step with time, meaning time by the clock and time in history; in other words: *nowadays* she was no longer what she had *once* been; a democrat, although, in addition to being called a 'scatterbrain', she was also known as a 'peacenik' who signed all sorts of petitions, the more obscure the better. Strange rumours circulated about her absent-mindedness: it was not only well known, not merely 'said' but confirmed by Dulber the locksmith, that Stollfuss, in order to keep her wayward fingers off the files he often brought home to study, had ordered a steel cabinet, 'a regular safe', for which he kept the master key and the sheriff's officer the spare. A number of things had happened which the *Rhineland Daily News* described as 'no longer merely *approaching* the scandalous': for example, the disappearance of certain documents to do with the case of Bethge, the perpetrator of an unsuccessful holdup at the Birglar National Bank; the documents in question turned up literally fifteen minutes before the trial opened. (Only Hollweg, her loyal and discreet nephew, the 'newspaper man', knew and never disclosed that it was he, together with Schroer, who had suddenly hit on the brilliant idea of searching the garbage dump between Kireskirchen and Dulbenweiler, where the recently unloaded garbage proved to Hollweg's surprise to be 'very easily identifiable'; there they found the Bethge files, Stollfuss's wallet containing eighty-five marks in cash, and all his papers and notes dealing with the conduct of the Bethge case. It had also been Hollweg who – in exchange for such bitter compromises as refraining from criticizing either the Christian Democrats or the Socialists – asked his newspaper colleagues to deal lightly with her, and succeeded because she also had the right connections 'in the city', with Grellber, for instance.) Sometimes, so Birglar people said, she would begin making the beds at nine in the morning, and then, when the clock struck noon, would wake up 'like Snow White from her trance', still holding the same sheet she had picked up at nine to smooth out or change.

To his surprise, when he called 'Maria' she emerged from the kitchen still wearing her apron – pale blue with pink bows – 'actually a bit too young for her', he always thought, although he never said so. There was a smell of – was it duck or turkey? – anyway, there was certainly a smell of stewed apples and rice;

she kissed him on the cheek and said, pleasantly excited: 'IT's arrived.'

'What has?' he asked in alarm.

'Goodness me,' she said in her pleasant voice, 'nothing from Grellber, don't worry – I mean your notice of retirement; the official ceremony is to take place in four weeks, and I bet they'll pin a medal on your chest or hang it around your neck. Aren't you pleased?'

'Oh yes, of course I am,' he said listlessly, kissed her hand and then stroked his cheek with it, 'I only wish I had been pensioned off yesterday.'

'But you shouldn't wish that, what would become of Gruhl? Acquittal, but with restitution – I've been saying so all along. Just imagine what would have happened if he'd got into the clutches of one of those super-democrats. Acquittal, that's what I say.'

'But you know an acquittal would be absurd.'

He preceded her into the dining-room, poured two glasses of sherry from a decanter, held hers out to her with an affectionate smile, and said: 'Cheers!'

'*Prost,*' she said, 'by the way, Grellber rang up five minutes ago. He agrees with me entirely.'

'Agrees with you?'

'Yes,' she said, finishing her glass and untying her apron. 'I believe he gave you the Gruhls because he knows how fond you are of acquitting. A parting gift. Why don't you accept it? Acquit them!'

'That's enough,' he said sternly, 'you know what an old fox Grellber is. An acquittal is out of the question. What else did Grellber want?'

'To know if there were any reporters there.'

'What did you say?'

'I told him there weren't any.'

'But how did you know?'

'I talked several times on the phone to Frau Schroer. Grellber had already called earlier this morning.'

'You mean he's called more than once?'

'Yes. Frau Schroer told me there wasn't a single reporter there, or anyone else making notes – Grellber seemed very relieved to hear it. But tell me, did you have to be so hard on Agnes? Send her some flowers.'

'Nonsense,' he said, 'that crazy female. She made things very embarrassing for me.'

'Send her some flowers, I say, and write on the card: "Forgive me! Affectionately, Alois."'

'Come on now, that's enough.'

'Well, I'm sure what Agnes did wasn't as embarrassing as the other thing Frau Schroer told me about.'

'You'd better not even tell me,' he said wearily, pouring himself some more sherry and holding out the decanter toward her; she declined.

'Very well then, I won't tell you.'

'Is it about the court?'

'Indirectly, yes.'

'Damn – all right, tell me!'

'I really think you should know. You might be able to do something about it.'

'Is it *very* bad, *very* annoying?'

'No, only funny and a *little* bit awkward.'

Her broad pale face, still pretty and childlike, although the contours were blurred, was puckered with amusement; she stroked his bald head with its ring of sparse grey hair, saying in a low voice: 'It's that – what's she called again? Eva, I believe, from the restaurant, the one who takes Menu Number Four across to them every day,' she giggled. 'She's spreading the news quite proudly: "I gave myself to him and have conceived from him": to use her own words.'

'Damn it all,' said Stollfuss, 'let's hope she's not a minor at least.'

'Just missed it. A sweet little thing.'

'But she's only been taking their meals over for the past six weeks.'

'That's just how long it takes to voice one's first proud suspicions – and they're usually right, incidentally.'

'I hope it was the boy, at least?'

'Yes, it was.'

'Seven or eight weeks ago Grellber gave them both leave to attend his father-in-law's funeral. She *must* be persuaded to say it happened then.'

'Just you try and persuade her.'

'Won't you?'

'I'll try all right – but it would be better to get the happy lover to try.'

'He's a sensible lad.'

'With a taste I can only admire – she's the prettiest little thing I've seen hereabouts.'

'Oh well, Hermes'll have to do it for me. By the way, you can order the flowers for Agnes by phone.'

'By phone? You ought to know by now that everyone around here considers the phone a quite legitimate source of information; they'll already know by now at the Jug of Beer that "a man's voice" agreed with what I said about the verdict, I mean about acquittal.'

They had their soup and main course (duck, after all, he was pleased to discover) in silence; he ate sparingly, she heartily. For forty years they had consumed their soup and main course – he sparingly, she heartily – in silence; he had first insisted on these wordless twenty minutes in the days when he had been a young district attorney; he needed this short respite to think about the next stage of the trial, and while she went into the kitchen to get the coffee and dessert he made some brief notes on a slip of paper: Horn? he wrote, St A.? Then Father K., old Frau L., Wermelsk.??, three sold., Grä, Ki, Ha; he numbered the abbreviations, then changed the numbers around so that Grä, Ki, Ha came before the soldiers.

This was something he could never have too much of: her freshly baked apple strudel with vanilla cream sauce, and the beautiful Meissen coffee-pot; for thirty years he had used this moment to warm his cold hands on the pot before quickly swallowing his heart drops from a liqueur glass; for forty years he had been looking at his wife's fair-skinned face, once blooming and now paler and broader, and had sat with her at this great walnut table which had been bought with numerous children, 'six at least', in mind. Instead: miscarriages that had left behind them not even the consolation of a grave, a place in the earth, but had vanished without trace in gynaecological clinics; doctors' bills, hormone injections, specialists' furrowed brows, until even the monthly hope was a thing of the past, and at the age of forty she had lapsed once more into the non-bleeding state of a ten-year-old girl and he had given up coming to her with his manhood; she was garrulous and forgetful, he was a boy again, though no longer tormented by the things that torment boys. Not even a place in the earth of a cemetery, and yet for forty years the two of them – he eating sparingly, she heartily – had been looking at the empty chairs as if expecting tears, bickering, whining, greed, or envy, and never once had it occurred to them to choose a smaller dining table. They seldom had guests; these empty chairs of the children who had never been born were obliged to remain standing around the table, even twenty years after she had become a little girl again; or would Sarah's miracle be repeated in her, so many years after she had ceased to function as a woman? In her mildly hysterical imagination she had made sporadic attempts to fill the empty chairs with fantasy dream-children, to forbid a daughter Monika to overeat, to encourage the appetite of a son Konrad – but he had refused to permit these occasional efforts, addressing her as if she were a sleepwalker in the calm, matter-of-fact voice with which he pronounced judgement in court; now and again she had tried setting places for these fantasy dream-children, though not very often, two or at most three times in forty years: he had removed the plates and glasses from the table with his own hands and smashed them in the garbage can in the kitchen, not brutally, not cruelly, but in a perfectly natural way, as if he were clearing files from the table, and she had not wept or cried out. She had merely nodded with a sigh, as if accepting a just sentence. There was only one promise he had made her and kept, a promise made even before he married her: never to be involved in a death sentence.

In other places, where she was a stranger and alone, places where he would never go, she apparently used to talk about a daughter who had died and a son who had been killed in the war; he found out about this just once, at the little pension in the Bavarian Forest where he was suddenly summoned after she had been taken to hospital with a sprained ankle. At breakfast the landlady asked about their son Konrad, a medical student who had fallen at the front near a town called Voronezh. From the lips of a stranger – with his wife not present – it sounded convincing, in fact it rang true: a fair-haired, dedicated young-ster who had picked up an infection in a typhus hospital and died in the arms of the young Russian girl he loved: why shouldn't that be true? Why shouldn't she choose as their son a fair-haired, dedicated youngster long forgotten by his own family and now not even a handful of dust? It seemed that when he was not with her she populated the earth with a de-ceased daughter and son, and then depopulated it again. That sad business about Monika, said the landlady, perhaps that had been more tragic still: killed in a plane crash on the way to her fiancé 'over there', the plans for the wedding all set; by 'over there' had his wife meant America, and if so, which – North, South, or Central America? Central, he said, stirring the sugar in his coffee; her fiancé had been waiting for her in Mexico, no, not a German, a Frenchman teaching at the university there. Mexico? University and Frenchman, mightn't he have been – she didn't want to pry, and after all it was none of her business – but mightn't he have been – a Communist? Of course she didn't want to offend him, for in her eyes Communists were human beings too; it was just that she was so concerned over the fate of their daughter after hearing so much about her from his wife, and she had read that people in Mexico were 'very leftist'; yes, he admitted, he had been a Communist, this young man, this Frenchman called Bertaud who had so nearly become his son-in-law. And he had never married anyone else, this Ber-taud, he was still faithful to the memory of Monika, killed in a plane crash off the west coast of Ireland; *this* was a game he enjoyed because it was not being played directly between the two of them and bore no relation to the fish-like creatures that had vanished without trace in the clinics of two small country towns and the city. This was the only time he found out about the game, the only time he had played it, for half an hour over breakfast, just before driving to the hospital to take her home in the ambulance. Her only wish was that, when the time came, she would die in the place where she had spent her childhood and be cared for by nuns who believed in the 'Son of the Virgin', one of whom was her sole surviving school friend – apart of course from Agnes, but friendship with her, 'sad to say', was unfortunately denied her; 'those two', she would say, meaning the nun and Agnes, 'their bodies would have borne children for you. Just look at their complexions: pigment, hormones. And their eyes – while mine become duller and paler all the time; one day, when I'm really old, they'll be as pale as egg-white.' Yes, those eyes of hers, they really were getting paler, like the blue on English postage stamps. But as for the children of this Irmgard and his cousin Agnes: no, no; possibly it was better to have none at all.

This was really one of her masterpieces, this fresh, crisp apple strudel; her unerring touch with the cinnamon and raisins, and the thick, rich sauce made of cream and vanilla – in gratitude he placed his hand on hers as it stirred his coffee for him.

'Tell me, have you ever heard of such a thing as a Happening?'

'Yes, I have,' she said.

He raised his eyes and gave her a stern look. 'Really, now, be serious.'

'But really,' she said, 'I am serious. You ought to read the national newspapers from time to time; a Happening is an entirely new art form, a new form of self-expression. They take some object and smash it to pieces, if possible with the consent of the owner, but if necessary without.'

He put down his dessert fork, raised his hands with that solemn gesture that filled her with alarm because it meant he was about to do something he rarely did – to exhort her, as if she were on the witness stand, to tell the truth, the whole truth, and nothing but the truth.

'But honestly, they do the strangest things, run cars down with locomotives, tear up streets, splash chicken blood all over the wall, smash valuable watches with hammers. . . .'

'And burn things?'

'I haven't read anything about burning, but why not if they pulverize watches and tear the arms and eyes out of dolls . . .?'

'Yes,' he said, 'why not set fire to something, if necessary without asking the owner's consent; why not place in my human hands a trial that should really be conducted before a jury; why not appoint an outsider as district attorney, and as court recorder a little man like Aussem who worships the God-dess of Justice (though perhaps not very ardently) and who – not so long ago – used to turn up every year at our door at carol-singing time with his runny nose and home-made lantern? Why not? Why not?' he said and, holding out his cup, to ask for more coffee, laughed heartily, boisterously, insofar as the cigar (still the same one he had started that morning) permitted boist-erous laughter. And when she seemed hurt because he did not – as they had always agreed to do – let her in on the joke that was even making him swallow cigar smoke, he said: 'Just think for a moment of your national dailies: jeep burns while litany sung and pipes knocked together in rhythm – can't you see why I'm laughing? Why Grellber doesn't want any reporters around and Kugl-Egger mustn't be allowed to see what it's all about?'

'Oh I see,' she said, taking a chocolate from the silver box and helping herself to coffee, 'of course I see now, those old foxes, although it sounds to me more like pop art.'

He liked that: when she lit a cigarette and puffed away like a ten-year-old trying to look depraved, that little white thing stuck jauntily in her mouth as if it were really a part of herself; forty years and no life kindled within her, not even a place in the earth, not even the memory of a single act of violence when he had come to her with his manhood; now they were children, grown very, very old. Once again he laid his hand on hers. 'I can't remember when I've enjoyed a meal more,' and he laughed again at the thought of his memo: Grä, Ki, Ha, three sold., Fa. K. – wasn't that almost an example of pop art in itself?

*

Seldom had he felt so free, so light of heart, on returning to a trial; he put on his hat and coat with a flourish, lifted his stick from the stand, and kissed his wife's pale round face, still puckered with amusement. Even Birglar seemed less stuffy, less narrow; it was really quite pretty, the way the Duhr, muddy and sluggish though it was, flowed through the little town, the pathway along its bank, the little rise with its look-out, the controversial war memorial, St Nepomuk's statue by the bridge, the east gate, the west gate, the 'maximum accident zones', 'traffic bottlenecks', even the red-and-white shutters of the town hall had their charm; what was wrong with living in Birglar and dying in Birglar?

'No, not roses,' he said at the flower shop, 'and not asters either' – not flowers of love or death. 'Yes, that'll do,' he said, 'that nice autumn bouquet – you know Fräulein Hall's address, I take it?'

At the Duhr Terraces the only thing to turn out a success was the chocolate parfait, which was served as a consolation and peace offering even to those customers whose choice of menu did not entitle them to it; it had been prepared the evening before, in quantities out of all proportion to the probable number of orders for Menu Number Four, by the hands of her whose proud announcement had so upset the heart, emotions, and skill of her mother that even her speciality – the sauerbraten – had been a failure. The parfait was served by her father who, subdued but not inconsolable, apologized for the disappointing meal with the words: 'There are emotional reasons involved which it would be too complicated to explain'; moreover, he collected payment in smaller amounts than were shown on the menu, even from Bergnolte, whom he did not like. Nor did he display any irritation when he was asked, twice within a short period and both times by the same male voice, to call customers to the telephone: on the first occasion the male voice had asked him whether there was a telephone booth there and, if so, whether it was sound-proof. So Kugl-Egger and Bergnolte were summoned in turn to the booth where each stayed quite a while, five or six minutes, maybe more; while the first was, if not shaken, still visibly upset when he emerged, the second wore a satisfied smile.

A slight delay occurred at about a quarter-to-three as everyone was getting ready to leave, when Hollweg came in, freshly bathed and in excellent spirits, waved to Hermes and Kugl-Egger, bowed to the ladies from a distance, and went over to the table at which Grähn, Frau Schorf-Kreidel, and Aussem were sitting, where he was advised to order ham and eggs or an omelette since everything else, even the salad, was uneatable. Keeping their voices low, Frau Schorf-Kreidel, Grähn, Hollweg, and Aussem, kindred spirits of the Liberal opposition, were discussing a talk to be given the following evening; it was hoped that Frau Hermes would not turn up there again and 'steal the show for the Catholics of Birglar County' with her irreverent *avant-garde* questions. 'That woman,' said Frau Schorf-Kreidel in an undertone, 'the best thing that could happen to us would be for her to be excommunicated.' While waving affably to Frau Hermes as the latter, arm in arm with Frau Kugl-Egger, left the terrace, she promised to go into the city that very afternoon and warn the lecturer about the heckling to be expected from Frau Hermes; this young member of the legislature was to speak on the subject of 'World Nutrition – Birth Control – The Welfare State', and it was to be expected that Frau Hermes, notorious for her dedication to the cause of 'The Pill', would jump with both feet into the fray. Anyway, Hollweg promised to attend himself, on behalf of his paper and to write an editorial which 'I faithfully promise will not contain as much as half a line about Else'. He asked casually how things were going with the Gruhl trial, whereupon Grähn described the witness-room as being quite lively; Frau Schorf-Kreidel said it was a pity that the only person who might have brightened things up a bit, Sanni Seiffert, had been summarily choked off. When she described how Gruhl had lighted up his pipe and, so to speak, scorched her, but, 'with his usual charm, you know how he is', apologized, Hollweg said it sounded quite delightful and could form

91

the basis of a nice little local sub-editorial on the subject of 'Smoking in the Courtroom'; here Aussem joined in and wondered whether, under the pseudonym of 'Justus', he might not write a short article on 'The Absurdity of Burning Automobiles and the Absurdity of Certain Courtroom Procedures', but Hollweg cut him short and whispered that 'our friends' had specifically requested that the trial be not written up, and even he would have to forgo his sub-editorial, since smoking in court, and especially 'by the accused', was a too easily recognizable misdemeanour.

On the way back to the court-house Hermes asked Kugl-Egger why he did not challenge the competence of the court and request a trial by jury at the very least, to which Kugl-Egger replied with a smile that no one disputed the defence attorney's right to challenge this 'admittedly' curious legal situation and to have the case transferred to Prell where he might get two years for his clients rather than six months (promptly corrected by the defence attorney to four months); but he doubted the success of such action, the charge being after all property damage and public mischief. He shrugged his shoulders, smiled ominously, and said it really wasn't much more than a case of smuggling, poaching, or 'moonlighting', with possibly some elements of blasphemy, for indeed the singing of the litany had been most improper. Where there was no plaintiff – and he, the district attorney, was the plaintiff – there was no judge. Hermes was more than welcome, if he felt like it, to demand a heavier sentence!

Frau Kugl-Egger, by this time quite upset and neither appeased nor duped by the chocolate parfait and excellent coffee offered to compensate for the disastrous meal, was somewhat relieved when they finally reached the courtroom, this being some sort of guarantee that Frau Hermes would be silent for at least the next few hours. She had begun to long for 'that little place east of Nuremberg': her home town seemed so unhomelike to her, and by now she was thoroughly and exhaustively familiar with Frau Hermes's opinions on the vital issues of the day; besides, she had meanwhile discovered that this woman really was that bouncing blonde girl who had seemed to be 'somehow forever chewing an apple' and who had had to be packed off to boarding school in a hurry for an extended period, all in all not a disagreeable person and certainly not bad at heart, just utterly exhausting, with tears always sounding through her high-pitched laughter. Had she been to Israel? Frau Hermes just had time to ask Frau Kugl-Egger as the court officials filed in; Frau Kugl-Egger was spared having to answer, could only shake her head, whereupon Frau Hermes just managed to indicate with inimitable gestures that she *must* go there, that was something one *must* see.

The lieutenant made up his mind to write off the first half of this day as a morning of misfortune during which – he was still hoping that his testimony during the afternoon would dispel at least some of his depression – everything had gone wrong or conspired to annoy him: his conversation with the priest, his attempt to keep his two subordinates in line as to both tact and morals, and now this fiasco of a meal, not really redeemed by the reduced price and the chocolate dessert. At first he had been inclined to regard the fiasco as a 'personal as well as ideological' expression of hostility toward himself and the institution so dear to his heart; but then, when the proprietor apologized and offered, in addition to the chocolate dessert, a free cup of coffee, 'to restore the house's reputation' which had been jeopardized 'by unforeseeable emotional problems', he had looked into those dog-like brown eyes with their lurking shrewdness: he expected to find mockery, but did not, so, partially consoled, he smoked a cigarette while he drank his coffee and finished reading the editorial in the national daily.

At the Café Frohn, before Frau Leuffen emerged from the kitchen to announce that it was time to return to the court-house, and after the Scholwens had made inordinate demands on Frau Wermelskirchen's advice, Frau Wermelskirchen had delivered herself of an uninhibited and dramatic life-story and, in barely twenty-five minutes, in addition to this confession, had extemporized for the benefit of the startled priest an almost complete philosophy of love: how she had married, or rather been married off, very young to Wermelskirchen, at that time a sergeant; he had begun by marrying her – she had been sixteen at the time, young, gay, hungry for life and love – 'in church with all the trimmings' and had then gone on to seduce her; it was terrible the things he had done with her, terrible, and it had scared her to find what sex can do to men. For two years she had been married to Wermelskirchen, a cunning, lazy fellow twice her age, thirty-two, but one thing for sure, a man: not a soldier, not a farmer, just a man, and that to such a degree and in such a way that it had reduced her to tears; but then during the final months of the war he had been sent to the front from Birglar, where he had a soft job in a transport unit, and two days later he was dead. One of his buddies had brought her the news, and what was more, he had known, and told her he knew, what her skin, her hands, were like; he had been as familiar with her body as the husband who, beyond death, had resumed possession of her through this fellow, 'a terrible betrayal', and that was the trouble: she wasn't Wermelskirchen's widow, she was still his wife; he still possessed her, the man who had long since been 'ploughed under' in some forest, with no grave, no cross, no earthly trace. Oh he was *alive* all right, no one had to tell her the dead aren't dead, but sometimes she felt it would be better if the dead really were dead; but when all was said and done she had been given to this Wermelskirchen by her devout parents before priest and altar, and couldn't he, the priest, understand how 'he sometimes wouldn't let go of her', this Judas who had even betrayed the little mole she had on her back and given it away to someone else? Soup and coffee grew cold, necessitating a long inept apology murmured to Frau Frohn when she came over to them with Frau Leuffen, although there was no need at all for this, Frau Frohn having immediately grasped that something exceptional had been going on here. 'He sat there,' she recounted later, 'holding her hand, the way lovers sometimes do at the movies, holding those exquisite hands of hers, and neither one of them so much as touched the soup or the coffee.'

Upstairs, where they met to put on their gowns again, Stollfuss informed the attorneys that, since he intended to conclude proceedings that day, he suggested they get their notes ready for their pleadings; he thought it might be possible to wind up the witnesses' testimonies, a further interrogation of the two Gruhls, and the two experts, Professor Büren and Motrik the art dealer, by six-thirty at the latest, with a recess at that point and perhaps even a short additional one before then. Kugl-Egger seemed very satisfied with this plan, but Hermes not particularly so; of course, he said, he was more than agreeable to this schedule, but he had some doubts as to whether his clients could stand up to 'such an ordeal'; however, all he got for this argument was a benign smile from Stollfuss and a mocking one from Kugl-Egger, and with a wry smile he accepted Stollfuss's friendly request to refrain from resorting to such familiar tricks as having his clients faint or collapse; it was always possible, said Stollfuss as they went downstairs, with a mildly threatening ring to his voice, it was always possible, if Hermes were really afraid of his clients' collapsing or fainting, to summon Dr Hulffen from St Mary's Hospital, so conveniently located only two minutes away. Frau Schroer was also prepared to give assistance. Hermes was expecting a visit late that evening from one of his wife's school friends who sometimes wrote articles for a national daily, and he had been secretly hoping to acquaint her with the legal quirks of the proceedings and persuade her to attend the trial the next morning; he now felt not just slightly but considerably out-manoeuvred, and was already thinking up possible grounds for an appeal.

Three

Of the morning's dozen spectators there now remained only three: Frau Hermes, Frau Kugl-Egger, and Bergnolte, who was wondering whether the meal in what had been recommended to him as the 'best restaurant in town' could really have been as bad as it seemed, or whether his impression was due merely to the 'state of his taste buds at the time'; he found it hard to believe that Grellber – who had such a reputation as a gourmet that he was sometimes called upon to testify, in an amateur capacity, at proceedings involving infractions of food laws – had not been serious when he had smacked his lips in retrospective pleasure as he recommended the cooking there. With these thoughts in mind he resumed his former seat, at first pleased, then somewhat uneasy at the thinning out of the row of spectators. Those who stayed away that afternoon were: the wife of Heuser, the traffic sociologist, who had to prepare a report for her husband on traffic-light problems (she had statistics to evaluate, notes to enter, and the outline of the report to draft); Agnes Hall, for reasons known to us; Leuffen, the Huskirchen butcher, Gruhl's brother-in-law, because he had to slaughter a pig and a calf for a big wedding the next day; two colleagues of Gruhl senior who had wanted to hear the auditor's testimony but who couldn't sacrifice their afternoon as well and so had asked Gruhl, via Schroer, to give them the highlights the next time they met; Frau Schorf-Kreidel, also for reasons known to us; and three old-age pensioners who usually spent only their mornings as 'students of crime' but their afternoons in a quiet back room of the Jug of Beer, practising for a Skat tournament that had been organized for the following Sunday in Wollershoven by the committee for the 'Entertainment of Our Senior

Citizens': these three – an old farmer, a retired schoolteacher, and a factory foreman of nearly eighty – all found, independently of one another, 'something funny about this business', but beyond that nothing particularly remarkable since they were familiar with the whole case.

There were only two new additions to the spectators: Huppenach, a young farmer who had formerly served in the army with the younger Gruhl and now lived in Kireskirchen, the next village, and who had to go to the country savings bank anyway to see about a loan, and a retired county council official by the name of Leuben who was distantly related to Stollfuss. Bergnolte's suspicion that these two were journalists was but a fleeting one; a swift appraisal of their manner and facial expressions was enough to dissipate such doubts immediately.

The palpably increased good humour of the judge and the accused deserved by rights a far larger body of spectators; the two Gruhls in particular, if they had seemed relaxed and at ease during the morning, now radiated a cheerfulness that even improved the somewhat impaired mood of the defence attorney. The fiasco of the midday meal did not seem to have soured the disposition of the district attorney; he had simply ordered a second dessert from Schmitz in the form of one of his famous *omelettes soufflées*; the Gruhls, Fortune's favourites, were the only Duhr Terraces customers who had not been affected by the disruption of the cuisine, the announcement precipitating this disruption not having been made by the young lady until the only perfect veal cutlets of the day were already on the Gruhls' tray. Gruhl senior had been inordinately stimulated by the coffee, which was of outstanding excellence that day, and with it had smoked one of those cigars – fragrant blend of perfect purity – which Schmitz, as he well knew, rarely 'shelled out' to anyone. Eva Schmitz's announcement that she was pregnant had placed both Gruhls, father and son, in a genuine state of euphoria: they had taken turns executing a little dance with their fiancée and daughter-in-law respectively and had asked her over and over again whether she was quite sure.

97

The district attorney, exhilarated by the fact that his colleague Hermes was evidently not going to have things all his own way, began by summoning Gruhl senior once again to the rail and asking him good-humouredly whether he had not been mistaken in stating that he had been in conflict with the law, the tax laws, but had no previous conviction. Gruhl said no, he had no previous conviction – except for the innumerable seizure orders . . . whereupon the district attorney interrupted him with a bland smile and said no, he didn't mean those. He was merely seeking an explanation for the odd fact that had struck him on rereading the files, the fact that, although he had not been called up until 1940, Gruhl had been made a sergeant-major by the end of 1942 but, strangely enough, had resumed the rank of private by the end of 1943. Oh, said Gruhl cheerfully, that was very easy to explain, he had simply been demoted during the summer of 1943. I see, said the district attorney, maintaining his genial manner, the accused seemed to take that very lightly; were all soldiers so casually demoted? No, said Gruhl, his cheerfulness now bordering on jubilation, he had had to submit to a court martial and had been sentenced to eight months' imprisonment, but had only had to serve six, in a kind of fortress confinement. At this point the defence attorney intervened sharply and asked the judge whether it was permissible in this court to describe a military sentence as a previous conviction. The district attorney replied that he had not yet *described* any military sentence as a previous conviction, and the judge replied calmly to Hermes that it depended on the offence for which Gruhl had been sentenced. With a smile the district attorney now asked Gruhl senior whether or not, if he were questioned about it, he would be prepared to reply. Without consulting his attorney, Gruhl nodded and said yes, he would be prepared to reply, at which the district attorney said: 'Then let us hear what happened.'

According to Gruhl, even during his basic training he had constantly been assigned to carpentry jobs, sometimes in the homes of officers and non-coms, sometimes in the battalion workshop; when his regiment moved to France after the end of the war there (question interjected by the district attorney: 'You mean the campaign in France?' Gruhl's reply: 'I mean the war') he had been first in Rouen and later in Paris. Because he was 'in such demand' he had been passed on to higher and higher levels, ending up working for a colonel, 'nothing but Louis XVI – it was a craze of his wife's'; later on a small carpentry shop in the Paris suburb of Passy had been requisitioned for him, only a small place but containing everything he needed; he had gone there every morning, done his work, and later taken to sleeping there. Still later he had made friends with a fellow carpenter, the owner of the workshop, and had persuaded the colonel to let this man work with him; his name was Heribault, and they were still good friends. Heribault now owned a thriving antique business; the idea of starting up a business of this kind had come to him while working with Gruhl during the war; Heribault had been an exceptionally good carpenter, mainly furniture, but not period furniture, which was something he, Gruhl, had taught him. Well, anyway, after a while Heribault had worked entirely for his own account; the colonel hadn't had the slightest suspicion, and naturally Gruhl had never enlightened him as to the length of time spent on a job; on a small chest of drawers which, working for himself, he would have taken a week or even three days to restore at home, he had spent up to two months. Well, one day he had told the colonel that at home he could easily earn up to five hundred marks a month doing work of this kind, and that the wages of a private were really a very poor recompense. The colonel had laughed, and he had then been very quickly promoted first to private first class, then to sergeant, and finally to sergeant-major. After a while groups had begun meeting at Heribault's workshop; a few men would come there of an evening, women too, bringing along wine and cigarettes, and each time Heribault had sent him away, saying it was better for them and for him if he knew nothing of the discussions going on; there had been a sign on the door: German Armed Forces, or some such thing. On those occasions he had always gone off to the movies or a dance hall and, at Heribault's request, had never got back till midnight. When the district attorney, with deceptive blandness, asked him whether he hadn't found that suspicious, Gruhl said, suspicious, no, but naturally he hadn't imagined the men and women met there to discuss the wording of a declaration of loyalty to Hitler. It was war, after all, and it hadn't been his impression that the French had been very enthusiastic about it. Heribault had helped him and the colonel to get hold of furniture; he had known a lot of carpenters and antique dealers, as well as private individuals. The furniture was paid for in butter, cigarettes, and coffee, 'in such quantities, in fact, that even the neighbours got something out of it'; any price was paid in butter, coffee, and cigarettes; he, Gruhl, had moved around a good deal, had gone to Rouen, Amiens, and later Orléans, always taking along little packages for Heribault's friends: butter, coffee, and so on, until one day Heribault had asked him whether he would take along a food parcel even if he knew it contained neither butter nor cigarettes nor coffee. Well, by this time he had become very good friends with Heribault – he had lived and taken his meals with the family, and Madame Heribault and their little girl had been very good to him when his wife died – so he asked Heribault to tell him what was in the parcel, and he had said, 'nothing very bad, just paper, but unfortunately printed with things which would hardly be to your colonel's liking'. Anyway, he had taken along the parcels, several times, until one day a soldier at headquarters, where he had to go from time to time to pick up his ration cards and pay, had whispered a warning to him that the workshop was being watched. He had in turn warned Heribault, who promptly cleared out with his family; Gruhl had been arrested two days later; he had admitted taking the parcels along, but not to knowing what was in them. After the trial, incidentally, they had clamped down on the 'whole furniture business – for that had been the main factor, as it turned out', and even the colonel had been demoted. When asked whether the sentence had seemed a just one to him and whether he had felt any remorse, Gruhl said no. He had felt no remorse at all; and as to whether the sentence had seemed a just one – well, 'just' was a big word,

and particularly awkward in terms of war and its consequences.
Oh, so he found the words 'just' and 'justice' awkward, did he?
– was that still the case? Yes, said Gruhl, 'downright awkward,
even today'. Hadn't he, the district attorney went on, claimed to
have no interest in politics? Why then had he helped these
people? Just because he wasn't interested in politics, that's why;
he had liked them, 'but that wouldn't make sense to you'. The
district attorney flared up and took exception to the accused's
pronouncing yet another judgement on his intelligence; anyway,
he had no further questions. The attitude of the accused was
now perfectly clear and, taken in conjunction with Horn's attitude, became even clearer; furthermore, he was struck by the
fact that the accused regarded the strangest things as 'natural';
he called everything 'natural'. The judge gravely reprimanded
Gruhl for his 'but that wouldn't make sense to you' and, no
longer in quite such excellent humour because he saw his pre-
cious time slipping away, permitted the defence attorney to put
a question to Gruhl. The defence attorney: what had Gruhl
done while in military confinement and after his release? Gruhl,
tired now, and losing interest: 'Repaired furniture, later on in
Amsterdam.' When asked by the defence attorney whether he
hadn't seen any action at the front, Gruhl replied: 'No, I
fought only on the furniture front, chiefly on the Louis XVI,
Directoire, and Empire fronts.' The district attorney asked that
the expression 'furniture front' be censured, claiming that it was
disparaging to the victims of the last war, including his own
father, who had *not* been killed on the furniture front. On being
told by the judge to comment on this justifiable objection, Gruhl
told the district attorney in a quiet voice that it was not his
intention to belittle the memory of the fallen; his own family
had lost a brother, an uncle, and a brother-in-law, and furthermore his closest boyhood friend, the farmer Wermelskirchen
from Dulbenweiler, had been killed. But the fact remained that
he, Gruhl, had merely fought on the furniture front, and he had
often discussed this with his brothers, his brother-in-law Heinrich Leuffen, and his dead friend Wermelskirchen – in fact his
friend Wermelskirchen, who had been an air-force non-com and

won several decorations, had told him: 'You just hold out on the furniture front.' In other words, the expression was not his, Gruhl's, but that of a soldier, the holder of several decorations, who had been killed at the front. He felt under no obligation to take it back.

The interrogation of Father Kolb of Huskirchen, who was close to eighty, was almost like a conversation between friends; at times it assumed the form of a theological seminar on a popular level; it also contained some elements of village gossip but, to the relief of the judge and the disappointment of Frau Hermes and Frau Kugl-Egger, little of that which had spread the priest's reputation far beyond Birglar County: little of the 'fiery, fearless eccentricity' which was inherent in his utterances but not in their articulation. Bergnolte, the only person there who did not know him (the Kugl-Eggers had tasted samples of his temperament when they had first called on him in Huskirchen), described him to Grellber that evening as 'a real eccentric, if you know what I mean'.

With a courtesy in which even the most uncharitable could not have found a trace of offence, the judge offered Kolb a chair, which Kolb, with a courteous dignity equally devoid of offence, declined.

The priest stated that he had known the older Gruhl, if not from earliest childhood, at least since he was ten; in those days he often used to go to Huskirchen to visit his aunt Wermelskirchen. He had known him well since he was sixteen and had begun 'courting Elisabeth Leuffen, later his wife'. He had always known Gruhl for a very hard-working, reliable man; helpful, rather on the quiet side, but that might have something to do with his painful childhood experiences. When asked about these by the district attorney, Kolb said he saw no reason to discuss them; it was all too easy for such things to be exploited. The district attorney, not daring to insist on this point, then asked the priest about Gruhl's religious attitude, whereupon Kolb almost began to show signs of his famous temperament by saying, in a somewhat louder tone, that he was testifying in a *secular* court and no one here had the right to ask such a question – a question, in fact, that he would not even answer before an ecclesiastical court, a question he had never answered. The judge instructed him courteously that he was indeed free to refuse to answer the question, but that the court was concerned to obtain a picture of Gruhl's character; since he, the reverend father, was after all a priest, it was perhaps not entirely unjustified to inquire as to this side of Gruhl's character. Kolb, his courtesy matching that of Stollfuss, disputed the connection between religion and character : in fact, he said, raising his voice again as he turned to the district attorney, he would even dispute the connection between religion and integrity. One thing he could say : Gruhl had *always* been a man of integrity; he had never spoken of religious matters in a derogatory or blasphemous manner, and as to secular matters, he had made himself very useful to the parish of Huskirchen during the rebuilding and refitting of the badly damaged church; he was also very fond of children and during the 'bad years' had made charming wooden toys with his own hands for the children who would otherwise have had no such Christmas gifts. Here Gruhl senior raised his hand for permission to speak; the judge granted it, and Gruhl said he wished at this point to volunteer the fact that he was indifferent to matters of religion and had been so for a long time, even in the days when he had received marriage instruction from the reverend father, some twenty-five years ago. In response to this the priest said it might well be that Gruhl lacked faith, but he regarded Gruhl as one of the few Christians in his parish. When the district attorney said, very politely, with something of a gracious smile, that he was rather surprised to hear such a statement from a priest, and – 'please, do forgive me' – that he had some doubts as to whether it was theologically tenable or acceptable and wondered if the priest didn't feel distressed by this indifference, the priest said, also politely, with something of a gracious smile, that many things in this world distressed him but that he didn't expect any alleviation of his distress by the state. As for the theological acceptability or tenability of his statement, the district attorney had probably 'had an overdose of Catholic societies'. The judge permitted himself a little joke by asking the district attorney whether he would care to summon some kind of theological expert to deal with Gruhl's religious convictions; the district attorney flushed, Aussem looked up and grinned, and later that evening he told his friends 'there was very nearly a row'. The defence attorney now asked the priest whether it was true that he had once found Gruhl smoking in church. Yes, said the priest, he had once, twice even, come upon Gruhl smoking his pipe in church; Gruhl – this was something he had evidently promised his deceased wife – sometimes came to sit for a while in church when there was no service going on, and it was true that he had found Gruhl sitting in one of the back pews smoking his pipe; at first he had been very shocked and angry and had looked on it as blasphemous, but then, when he saw the expression on Gruhl's face, had spoken to him, perhaps chided him gently, he had seen that his face wore an expression of 'almost innocent piety'. 'He was daydreaming, miles away in spirit, and you know,' the priest went on, 'maybe only a pipe-smoker, like myself, can understand that; a man's pipe becomes almost part of his body. I have caught myself entering the vestry smoking my pipe and not noticed I had it in my mouth until I pulled the chasuble over my head and the pipe got in the way of the narrow collar; and – who knows – if the sacristan hadn't been there, and if the collar hadn't been so narrow, perhaps I would have gone to the altar with my pipe in my mouth.' This remark of the priest's provoked a variety of reactions among court officials, accused, and spectators: Frau Kugl-Egger said later she couldn't believe her ears, Frau Hermes found it 'marvellous', and Bergnolte told Grellber that evening: 'I think he really must have gone a bit soft in the head'; the judge, the defence attorney, and the accused grinned; the district attorney told his wife that evening that he had felt decidedly queer, while young Huppenach laughed out loud and old Herr Leuben shook his head and said afterward that the priest had 'certainly gone too far'. When asked by the defence attorney what information he could give about Georg Gruhl, the priest, turning with a smile toward Gruhl junior, said that this one he really had known since he was a baby; he had been born in Huskirchen, had been baptized at home at his dying mother's request, and had gone to school in Huskirchen; in short, he knew him well. He took more after his mother but was 'wilder than she had been', a good, hard-working boy, absolutely devoted to his father; during his early years he had been brought up by his grandmother, then, after the war, when he was about three, by his father. There had been no change in Georg until he joined the Bundeswehr. Moreover, the fact that just at that time his father was getting deeper and deeper into trouble, but more than anything else 'the boredom, the unutterable boredom', had profoundly affected this fine, wholesome youth who had been so hard-working and so full of life; it had altered him, 'made him resentful, vindictive almost'. The district attorney politely but firmly interrupted the priest at this point, saying that anyone who became resentful or vindictive while serving in a democratic institution such as the Bundeswehr – although, in view of the attitude, career, and whole philosophy of Gruhl senior as revealed here, it did not surprise him – anyone, therefore, who became vindictive in the Bundeswehr must have already had a certain predisposition; so his question to the reverend father was, how had the younger Gruhl's vindictiveness manifested itself? The priest, as firm and polite as the district attorney, denied the latter's thesis of a certain predisposition being necessary for a young man to become resentful or vindictive as a result of his military service; nothing could have a worse effect on a young man than insight into and experience of a giant organization of this kind, the whole point of which was the production of absurd futilities, of virtually total nothingness, in other words, which was pointless – well, that was how he saw it, and for that matter he must himself have a predisposition toward vindictiveness: in 1906 he had served one year as a volunteer in the artillery, and this experience of army life had 'sorely tempted him toward nihilism'. As for the district attorney's main question about *how* young Gruhl's vindictiveness had manifested itself, well, to begin with, Gruhl, who as a boy had gone regularly to church without being particularly devout, and started making derogatory remarks about the Church in discussing a superior officer who was evidently somewhat too Catholic. Gruhl junior had told him that he, the priest, had no idea of 'the things that went on out there'. The only preacher he had ever heard was the priest; he had received his religious instruction from him, and he suggested that the priest founded the 'Catholic Church of Huskirchen'. However, young Gruhl's vindictiveness had also found an outlet in paintings and carvings that were little short of blasphemous; and once when he and his father had spent a week-end restoring a group of three carved wooden figures which included the Virgin Mary and which he had delivered to Frau Schorf-Kreidel on the instructions of an art dealer, he had attached an obscene quotation from the classics to the carving and signed it 'Your Mother of God'. With delicate irony the district attorney remarked that the expression *too* Catholic as applied by a reverend father to an officer of the Bundeswehr did strike him as a little strange, as did the reverend father's attitude toward a democratically conceived institution that was designed to defend those very values which the Church, whose doctrine differed from the reverend father's interpretation, must be concerned to maintain; he himself regarded these statements as emanating from a delightful eccentricity; what he could not understand at all, however, was the implication : the army as the equivalent of a school of nihilism. Surely it was common knowledge that such an institution was dedicated to order and discipline. The priest, without asking leave to speak, turned toward the district attorney and said in polite, even cordial tones that his statements did not emanate from any delightful eccentricity : on the contrary, they were theologically indisputable; what he, the district attorney, described as the Church's doctrine had evolved from the necessity of coming to terms with the powers of this world, and it was not theology but compromise. He had advised young Gruhl to refuse to do his military service, but Gruhl had said you could only do that for reasons of conscience, and his conscience was of no importance in this matter since it was not really involved in military service. What was involved was his reason and his imagination, and to tell the truth he, the priest, had realized that this young man's words contained a deep insight, for he didn't think much of conscience either; it could so easily be manipulated and changed into sponge or stone, whereas reason and imagination were divine gifts to Man. So he hadn't been able to offer much comfort to young Gruhl because he had seen for himself *how* grotesquely these two divine gifts, human reason and imagination, were handled; besides, one must not overlook the absurdity of the situation in which young Gruhl found himself, his father getting deeper and deeper into trouble while he, the son, was working for a pittance in mess halls, making furniture for bars; the worst thing, of course, had been this jeep trip, about which he ... Here the priest was gently interrupted by the judge and requested not to comment on this aspect, since it was to be dealt with at proceedings from which the public would be excluded and at which Gruhl's former superior officer was to testify. The old priest clapped his hand to his forehead and exclaimed: 'Oh, him – but of course, fancy my overlooking that! In my young days he'd have made an atheist of me in no time at all.' Then he added that surely there was nothing mysterious about this jeep trip, the whole village knew about it. The judge pointed out the difference between a whole village knowing about a certain matter, i.e., finding out about it through careless talk (turning toward the district attorney he asked, with a hint of sarcasm, whether the district attorney was considering a charge of betrayal of official secrets), and a trip made while on duty, and therefore in fact a secret mission, being dealt with publicly. 'If,' he said politely, 'we discuss this publicly, this trip, made while on duty, would become something which the gossip of three or four villages can never make it: it would become "official", i.e., "*officially* exposed to public debate"'; this was what distinguished such proceedings from rumour and gossip, regardless of how true or false these latter might be. He was therefore obliged to exclude Gruhl junior's jeep trip from this stage of the proceedings; at this point Huppenach, one of the remaining spectators, laughed so long and so loud that, after receiving stern looks from Schroer, he was reprimanded by the judge and had to be threatened with expulsion from the courtroom. Huppenach turned his laugh into a smile, described by the district attorney as disdainful and insubordinate; the judge said that, although he found Huppenach's smile 'not very respectful', he could not, in view of the lack of time at his disposal, bring himself to undertake a detailed analysis and moral evaluation of the smiles of spectators. When asked what comment he had to make on the priest's testimony, Gruhl junior replied evenly and still quite cheerfully that he thanked the priest for having described his mental and spiritual states so accurately and saving him the trouble of trying to describe them himself, something which he most certainly would have done with less accuracy than the priest. He had nothing to remove from or add to this testimony, the priest, who had indeed known him all his life and whom he greatly respected, having said everything which he could not have said nearly so well himself. The priest was dismissed with thanks. He committed a breach of protocol by embracing young Gruhl and expressing the hope that he might rediscover an objective in life at the side of a beloved and charming wife, whereupon Gruhl said with a broad smile that this was already the case. The judge's rebuke of the priest's embrace was a very mild one and sounded almost like an apology.

During the brief recess Stollfuss asked the attorneys to consider sacrificing one witness each; everything was so straightforward, couldn't they at least dispense with the two ladies, Frau Leuffen and Frau Wermelskirchen? After a moment's reflection the two attorneys consented, and the priest was now able to start for home accompanied by his two parishioners, who were simultaneously relieved and put out. Frau Kugl-Egger made use of the recess to leave the courtroom and keep an appointment with the decorator in her new Huskirchen apartment, to discuss the colour for the built-in kitchen cupboards. In her desire to recapture something of the rural atmosphere of 'that little place east of Nuremberg' to which her thoughts turned so nostalgically, she decided to walk and remembered a short cut she had often taken as a little girl – along the far side of the cemetery, through some low bushes, and then by the banks of the Duhr; this brought her face to face with the priest and the two ladies from Huskirchen. She was identified as 'Grabel's Marlies', and blushed a little when obliged to reply to this friendly childhood greeting in tones overlaid with a strong Bavarian accent; the priest playfully called her a 'traitor to her country' and advised her not to depend on Gruhl for carpentry work in her new home but to ask Herr Horn for his advice; Gruhl wouldn't even look at ordinary domestic carpentry any more.

Grähn, the next witness, gave his occupation as assistant professor of political economy, his age as thirty-two, and, in reply to the judge's question, stated that, yes, he had already been called in a number of precedents as an expert witness. With his thick fair hair and pleasant face, Grähn seemed more like a nice up-to-date young doctor; the long wait – particularly when combined with a tiring philosophical discussion with the lieutenant in the witness-room – had left him rather subdued and in none too good a humour, and on being told by the judge to comment in as few words as possible on the economic situation of the accused Gruhl senior, he replied, with that slightly mocking arrogance of the specialist, that if he was to give a professional opinion he could not guarantee for the length or brevity of his testimony. Although some cut-and-dried formulas did exist, a case such as this belonged 'almost to an antediluvian era of economics'. He must, therefore, request ... Yes, said the judge, by a 'few words' he had only meant as few as possible, not a distorting condensation. Grähn, who spoke without notes and even quoted his figures from memory, looked at neither the judge nor the accused nor the spectators; instead his gaze seemed to be focused on an invisible desk, or dissecting table on which a rabbit was awaiting his skilful hands; the hand movements with which he punctuated certain sections seemed to chop the air, but not in any cruel or brutal way. He had, he said, studied Gruhl's balance sheets and, with his consent, his income tax statements; he could only say, without further ado, that, as far as his financial plight was concerned, Gruhl was the victim of a relentless, remorseless, but – here he turned to Gruhl with a friendly gesture of apology – 'but, as I see it and even teach it, a necessary' process, one which was not even confined to our day but of which there had been many instances in the history of economics, for example during the transition from the medieval guild society to our modern industrial society, and again in the nineteenth century; in short: objectively speaking, it was impossible to halt this process, for in economics there was no such thing as a museum for subsidized anachronistic occupations. *That* took care of the economic aspect of the matter. The moral aspect was something he preferred not even to mention, since there were no moral aspects to modern economics; in other words: it was a state of battle. The relationship between income tax department and taxpayer was also a state of battle, with the tax legislation throwing out paragraphs as bait 'the way you throw a glove to the wolf chasing your sleigh, although not,' Grähn remarked with a smile, 'to distract his attention but to catch him'. Morally speaking, then, there was also nothing wrong with Gruhl's attitude, for his only fault lay in letting himself be caught, and that was not a moral fault. There was a philosophy of law but not of taxation; tax legislation favoured the cows that gave the most milk by not slaughtering them prematurely: applied to Gruhl, this meant that cows of his type occurred so rarely that tax laws handed them over to slaughter, when necessary to forced slaughter. In figures that a layman could understand, the picture was roughly as follows: a business such as Gruhl's worked with far too low expenses because hardly any machinery and very little material were necessary; what brought in the money were his hands, his skill, and his instinct. The result, seen both subjectively and objectively, was the most ridiculous balance sheets imaginable; for example during one year when his son was still working with him, Gruhl had had a turnover of, believe it or not, 45,000 marks, but during that same year could only prove expenses of 4,000 marks, which meant a net profit of 41,000 marks, income tax of approximately 13,000 marks, church tax of a further 1,300, sales tax of almost 1,700; i.e., including compulsory insurance, a total taxation of more than fifty-five per cent. Put simply, therefore, only 45 pfennigs, in fact in one other year only 35 pfennigs, of every mark earned should have found their way into Gruhl's pocket, whereas – again put simply – Gruhl had regarded seventy to seventy-five pfennigs of each mark as his 'honest earnings' and had spent accordingly. This, felt Grähn, should suffice to outline Gruhl's financial situation. He only begged to be allowed to draw one more comparison : a net profit of forty thousand marks in a business operated by 'two keen, hard-working, talented people' – in many cases that kind of net profit was not even achieved by a fair-sized operation with a turnover of almost a million marks; he was citing these comparative figures merely to show, 'in a readily understandable manner', how 'subjectively absurd' but objectively relentless and remorseless was the manner in which the national economy and tax legislation dealt with businesses that are 'anachronistic' and unable to follow the generally accepted principle of expanding investment and personnel costs, i.e., the whole expense structure. The subjective absurdity, popularly regarded as unfair, of the Gruhl case could perhaps only be compared with that of an artist who – he was citing merely imaginary, not statistically established values – produced a picture at a 'cost' of say, two to three hundred marks and then sold it for twenty to thirty thousand marks or more. Gruhl had not even had a telephone, he had paid no rent, and his only expenses had been that small quantity of material necessary for his work; he had not even had 'entertainment expenses', for naturally it was he who had been entertained by customers and art dealers since it was not he who was seeking their custom but they who were seeking his work. Another word or two and he would have finished with his testimony, said Grähn. He just wanted to explain quickly something which a layman probably found hard to understand : how Gruhl could have accumulated tax arrears of – it really was an astounding figure – 35,000 marks, or, including the seizure and interest costs, 60,000 marks. In the last five years alone, Gruhl had had a turnover of 150,000 marks, a net profit of 130,000 marks; if you calculated half of that, including all expenses, for taxes, and again half for what Gruhl had 'erroneously put into his own pocket', this enormous sum was easy to explain. During the latter part of his statement, which he delivered briskly and rapidly, Grähn had several times looked across at Gruhl with a strange expression of mingled pity and admiration. In conclusion he wished to add that modern tax policies no longer had much to say about tax morality; although this concept did still crop up from time to time, it was, in Grähn's opinion, basically absurd, and even untenable; the end result of tax policies was the creation of expenses that must appear ludicrous from any ethical point of view, and if he, Grähn, had to decide on Gruhl's guilt or innocence – in terms, of course, of his conduct in tax matters and not the incident which was the subject of the present proceedings – he would say: from a human standpoint absolutely innocent, and ethically too. Indeed even from the standpoint of abstract ethics there was nothing reprehensible in Gruhl's behaviour; but the fact remained that the economic process was relentless and remorseless, and financial legislation could not afford 'anachronistic court jesters', since it was obliged to regard net profit as net profit and nothing but net profit. 'I am not,' said Grähn (whose slim youthful appearance made a strikingly intelligent and agreeable impression, and who was now pointing his finger at Gruhl, not threateningly but indicatively), 'I am not a judge, I am not a priest, I am not an income tax official; I am an economic theoretician. As a human being I cannot but profess a certain respect for the accused: how, in view of his book-keeping practices, he has managed to continue to exist for more than ten years without getting into considerably more serious difficulties – as an economic theoretician I find myself confronted by this case, well, as a pathologist might be confronted by a case of incurable cancer, where death would have been expected five years earlier.' To the district attorney's question – whether, as a theoretician who, far from just setting out on his career, was obviously already in established practice, he could so categorically reject the aspect of tax morality – Grähn replied with some asperity. Of course this term was still in use; but he rejected the concept of morality in the *theory* of taxation and taught this principle publicly and in a position financed by the state. No further questions being asked, Grähn was excused.

During the brief interval that ensued while the next witness – Hubert Hall the bailiff – was being called, the fourth of the four remaining spectators, Leuben the retired county council official, slipped out of the courtroom: he had found Grähn's lengthy statement inordinately fatiguing and tedious and did not expect either Hall or Kirffel to be any less tedious. Huppenach was yawning too; he stayed on merely because he had not yet grasped the fact that the public was going to be excluded during the taking of the lieutenant's and the sergeant's evidence.

Hubert Hall the bailiff, aged sixty, whose thick dark hair stuck out as usual because he was always running his hands through it, made 'a contradictory impression'. As Bergnolte – the only one among those present who did not know Hall – told Grellber later on, 'I'd be inclined to say he seemed not only ambiguous but positively obscure; he was sloppy, absent-minded, and one could hardly call him confidence-inspiring.' When asked by the defence attorney whether he would be able to separate the personal from the official elements in describing his relations with the accused, Hall replied with almost brusque nonchalance that he was quite familiar with such schizophrenia, considering that his relations with most of his 'clients' were based on this dual footing. As to the personal side, he had 'of course' known Gruhl very well and got along splendidly with him, in fact had often had a beer with him; on such occasions *he* had usually invited Gruhl because, since he already held a 'writ of personal search and seizure' against him, he would have found it embarrassing to have to go through Gruhl's wallet and brief-case in order to seize any available assets. 'We're human

113

too, you know!' exclaimed Hall, and that was why, because he was human, he had always paid for Gruhl's drinks whenever they met. On being asked by the defence attorney for a definition of 'personal search and seizure', since he assumed this would be appropriate here, Hall read aloud from the instructions to bailiffs that he evidently always carried with him: 'The bailiff may search the clothes and pockets of the debtor. This does not require a special warrant. The body-search of a female will be entrusted by the bailiff to a reliable female person.' These instructions, said Hall, on whom the breathless hush in the courtroom seemed to have a soothing effect, were based on Paragraphs 758 and 759 of the Rules of Civil Procedure, which ran as follows:

Paragraph 758, Section (1): The bailiff is authorized to search the dwelling and depositories of the debtor insofar as this is required for execution of the judgment. Section (2): He is authorized to have locked house doors, room doors, and depositories opened. Section (3): When confronted by resistance, he is authorized to use force and may request police support for this purpose. Paragraph 759: In the case of resistance during execution of judgment, or if during the proposed execution neither the debtor nor a member of the debtor's family nor an adult person in the service of this family is present in the debtor's dwelling, the bailiff is required to call in two adult persons or a civic employee or a local police officer as witnesses.

Since Stollfuss neither interrupted nor questioned him, Hall, who appeared surprised by the fixed attention given to the reading of a text that was so familiar to him, resumed his testimony. In a plaintive voice reinforced by a certain display of pathos, he told the court how often he had been forced to subject 'certain ladies to personal search and seizure' in low dives known only too well to the law. The procedure usually consisted in stripping the shoes from their feet at just the right moment, 'since that's where, following an old tradition, most of them still keep their cash'; then he would quickly shake the contents of the shoes into a paper bag kept at hand for the purpose and leave before the procurer could be alerted; when he made these 'personal searches', said Hall, he was usually accompanied by a certain Frau Schurz. She had been a wardress in a women's prison for fifteen years and was up to all the tricks, including hiding-places in underwear, as well as being a 'woman of considerable physical strength'; he must admit, however – and the courts were well aware of this – that he had his troubles with Frau Schurz: she was – and this was why she had been dismissed from prison service – 'inclined to be rough'. In any case, said Hall, personal searches were a sickening business; he frankly admitted that he usually did his best to get out of them, but unfortunately there were some creditors who regarded him as their flunkey and insisted on their rights.

As for the personal aspect, Hall said in weary, almost indifferent tones, everyone in the town and county of Birglar knew – and he had a wider circle of clients than many prophets of the 'economic miracle' would care to admit – everyone knew he wasn't a monster and that he simply enforced the law, seizing property, sometimes of course with the aid of the police. As far as Gruhl was concerned, there had never been hard feelings between them. (Gruhl confirmed this by calling out: 'That's right, Hubert, I've never held anything against you!' and was sharply reprimanded by the judge for interrupting.) It was not so much a battle situation as a hunter-and-hunted situation, where the hunter had to use as many tricks as the hunted, but it was the hunted who had the advantage, if he was smart enough, because he was not bound by laws and regulations and could, as it were, move freely around the hunting-ground; whereas he, the hunter, was under strict observation and had to watch his step. When Stollfuss told him with unexpected asperity to keep to the point and not 'meander off into vague metaphors', Hall put his hand in his pocket and took out 'a grubby, incredibly crumpled, and quite improbable-looking piece of paper', as Bergnolte described it later to Grellber, and proceeded to read off some examples.

Late-payment fines alone, not counting execution costs, demands for payment, and postage, could bring tax arrears of 300 marks up to 552 marks in seven years and to 660 in ten years, i.e., well over double. Where large amounts were involved – as had happened in the Gruhl case – say, with an amount of 10,000 marks, in ten years the arrears would amount to 22,000 marks. If in addition there were tax *penalties* – as had also been the case with Gruhl, who had not only continued to be behind with his taxes but was also guilty of tax evasion – then, well then.... Hall let out a long, long sigh that seemed as if it would never end and of which Bergnolte later maintained that 'the whole courtroom had smelled of it'. Naturally, Hall went on to say, the demand and execution costs formed a special category dependent on the frequency of the demands for payment and the frequency of the seizures requested. Some creditors, of course, were so vindictive that, although they knew there was 'nothing to be got out of' a debtor, they demanded repeated seizures and thereby senselessly increased the debt; this was especially noticeable in the case of small amounts, the minimum seizure fee being one mark and the minimum demand-for-payment fee eighty pfennigs plus postage and it was no trick for a debt of, say, fifteen marks to increase within a few years by two, three, or even four times. There was the case of Frau Schmälders, a widow whose husband, as everyone knew, had been a waiter of decidedly bad reputation; this Frau Schmälders.... He was interrupted by the judge and asked to confine his testimony to the legal proceedings against Gruhl as they related to resistance against forced seizure. Hall said that actually it had not been a case of resistance against forced seizure; Gruhl had gone about it much more cleverly than that. Toward the end he had worked only in exchange for food items that virtually defied seizure and which, when they were in fact seized, really caused nothing but trouble : as an example, for restoring an antique wardrobe Gruhl had accepted forty pounds of butter, of which he had surrendered thirty-six pounds to Hall; Hall had been foolish enough to accept them, but during the night there had been a heavy thunderstorm, the butter had 'turned rancid on the spot', and of course had not only depreciated but become worthless; then Gruhl had threatened to sue him 'for improper storage of seized foodstuffs'. The

116

same sort of thing had happened with some hams, and he had had similar trouble with the present lessee of the Duhr Terraces, Herr Schmitz, for whom Gruhl had done a carpentry job, a big job, worth a lot of money – to be precise, a complete refurbishing of the restaurant, outstanding in its artistic value and greatly admired by all the customers. At first Gruhl had said it was a gift to Schmitz, an old friend of his, but he hadn't got away with that since a man in Gruhl's position was not free to make such valuable gifts; then he had come to an arrangement with Schmitz whereby for two years he would consume ten marks' worth of food and drink every day for lunch in the restaurant – that being the approximate value of the work done – but that was no good either. A man in Gruhl's legal position was restricted to a subsistence minimum, and that did not provide for ten-mark meals; so then Gruhl had arranged 'daily board, including breakfast, lunch, and supper for two years' for himself and his son. Although Schmitz had charged the Gruhls the equivalent of a subsistence minimum, he had served them meals worth several times that much, and – as was well known to the court – was continuing to provide them with such meals while they were in custody; in return, Gruhl had reduced the fictitious bill to a quarter. The matter was still pending; experts were engaged in estimating the true value of Gruhl's work, although, legally speaking, this was not nearly as complicated as it might appear. Anyway, in spite of all these tricks and dodges on Gruhl's part – 'after all, Herr Stollfuss, when you go hunting you get no kick out of a rabbit that walks in front of the muzzle of your gun, waiting meekly to be shot down' – *personally* he was still on the best of terms with Gruhl. The judge rebuked him again for the hunting metaphor which, 'in its human, and particularly its legal, application, seemed to him decidedly macabre and ill-chosen', and gave permission for the witness Hall to be cross-examined; the defence attorney declined, and the district attorney merely muttered indistinctly, but just audibly, that 'quite enough had been said' – following this up with something that sounded like morass and corruption.

*

117

There was an unforeseen incident during the hearing of the next witness, Kirffel the income tax inspector, who gave his age as fifty-five. Kirffel, a gentle, peace-loving man, had already made up his mind to demonstrate – although everything about him made it unnecessary for him to demonstrate – that he was 'not a monster' either. Kirffel, who was known throughout the whole county of Birglar as a connoisseur of painting and good books, a model of amiability and humanity; of whom tales had been told – although he strove to deny such rumours – that in some cases he had given money out of his own pocket, with no thought of repayment, to foreign workers who had tangled with the law, either because they had difficulty in meeting instalment payments or owed taxes on wages they had earned 'on the side'; Kirffel, whose nickname 'good old Hans' never carried even the slightest trace of irony: this was the man who, after so much unnecessary verbiage had gone unchallenged, was interrupted – scolded – after his very first sentence, and with a curtness that everyone, even the district attorney, found unwarranted. The trouble was that his first words had been: 'After all, we're only doing our duty.' 'Duty!' Stollfuss shouted. 'Duty? I should hope we all do our duty. I want no declamations here, I want facts!' Then Kirffel, to everyone's surprise, lost his temper and shouted back: 'I'm bound by the laws too, and I have to apply those laws, and what's more,' he unexpectedly added, his voice beginning to fade away, 'what's more, I know quite well I never went to university.' At which point he fainted. A brief recess was called in a broken voice by Stollfuss, who apologized to all those present, including Kirffel, while Schroer went to get his wife, who was experienced in such situations.

Kirffel was carried by Schroer and Gruhl – who was neither excused for this purpose nor even rebuked by the district attorney for his protocol-defying departure – Kirffel was carried into the Schroer kitchen, where Frau Schroer restored him to consciousness by rubbing his chest and legs with vinegar. Stollfuss was about to make use of the respite for a few puffs on his cigar but then felt ashamed because he really had a very high opinion of Kirffel and had been shocked by his sudden outburst. He followed the others into the kitchen, where Schroer and Gruhl were addressing words of comfort to Kirffel, while Frau Schroer had taken the opportunity to remove a cake from the oven and test its quality by piercing it with a hairpin. Stollfuss again apologized to Kirffel, following this with a short consultation in the corridor with Hermes and Kugl-Egger, who both agreed to dispense altogether with Kirffel as a witness. More than almost anyone else in Birglar, more even than his father the police inspector, Kirffel enjoyed the undivided affection of all sections and levels of the community.

It was just five-thirty when proceedings were resumed. The judge announced that he was now obliged to exclude the public because he was about to hear the evidence of Gruhl junior's former superior officers and fellow soldier; he was doing so at the request of the district attorney, who regarded any divulging of official secrets as a threat to national security. Only Frau Hermes and young Huppenach were affected. Frau Hermes did not mind very much: she was longing for a cup of coffee and a good gossip with her friend, a schoolteacher's wife who had joined the conspiracy to enliven the functions of the Catholic Academic Society by introducing modernistic ideas and who was now on the committee in charge of preparations for the St Nicholas ball. The only one who felt annoyed, and expressed his annoyance by shouting 'Oh shit!' was young Huppenach, who had been itching to see Lieutenant Heimüller and Sergeant Behlau publicly humiliated. He left the courtroom under protests which went unheeded. As soon as Huppenach and Frau Hermes had gone, Stollfuss announced that the third spectator, Counsellor Bergnolte, was not to be considered a member of the public since he was there in an official capacity. Neither the defence attorney nor the district attorney had any objection to Bergnolte's presence.

When the first military witness, Private First Class Kuttke, appeared, he was crimson in the face; after Kirffel, the last civilian witness, had been called, a violent dispute had broken out in the witness room among the lieutenant, the sergeant, and Kuttke, during which Kuttke had defended what he called his 'sexual freedom' in a loud yet somewhat querulous voice. Surprisingly enough, Kuttke's rather tortuous intellectuality had driven even the sergeant over to the lieutenant's side; the expression 'sexual freedom' irritated him, and he had a different way of describing the problem: 'The Minister of Defence has no authority over my private parts,' but the lieutenant disputed this, saying that the Bundeswehr needed the *whole* man. Kuttke, on the other hand had insisted that as a soldier of the Bundeswehr not only was he not (and it was this double negative that finally earned him the reputation of an intellectual) under any obligation to Christian morality, but the fact remained that it was this very Christian morality which the lieutenant was trying so hard to promote that had tolerated bordellos for two thousand years, and he must insist on his right to deal with a whore on her own terms (it had come out during the conversation that he had a date with Sanni Seiffert for the coming week-end). So it was with a flushed face that he entered the courtroom; moreover, due to his extreme mental and physical excitment, he had had to put on his glasses too quickly to wipe them properly, and they had got steamed up so that he stumbled over the threshold, just managing to catch himself before he mounted the witness stand. (Later that evening Bergnolte reported to Grellber that he had not exactly impressed him as a model soldier, which in turn caused Grellber to call up Kuttke's battalion commander, Major Troeger. When asked how types like Kuttke came to be accepted Troeger replied: 'We take what we can get, we've no alternative.') Kuttke, short, spare, almost skinny, looked more like an intelligent pharmacist who feels out of place working in a drugstore; he gave his age as twenty-five, his occupation as soldier, his rank as private first class. When asked by Stollfuss how long he had been in the army, he said four years; how was it, then, that his rank was still so low? Kuttke: he had once been a staff corporal but had been demoted over an awkward business involving some internal army matters; when asked for details, he begged leave to describe the affair briefly as 'woman trouble involving officers and other ranks'; he did not feel free to say more. Stollfuss then asked him why he had enlisted. He replied that he had graduated from high school and begun to study sociology, but later had heard about the money to be made in the Bundeswehr; taking the army's leisurely work tempo into consideration as well, he had decided to enlist for at least twelve years, at the end of which he would be thirty-three, receive a nice fat severance allowance – quite apart from being able to put aside some money before that – and would then open a betting office. Stollfuss, who oddly enough did not interrupt him, shook his head a few times during this statement, muttered 'hm, hm' or 'I see,' ignored the gesticulating of Bergnolte, who was sitting behind the accused, likewise the pencil-tapping of the district attorney, and let Kuttke carry on with his evidence. What he had in mind, said Kuttke, was to make betting on dogs popular in the Federal Republic; 'due to the inevitable advance of automation and the resultant shortening of work hours', the 'Federal German', as Kuttke called him, needed new 'stimulants'. Football pools and lotteries had degenerated into mere routine, and anyway he felt that mere number-games lacked magic or any sort of mystical quality; so the 'Federal German' must be offered other distractions. Kuttke, by this time 'quite himself' again, now seemed almost like a very intelligent, rather confused high-school student who had been caught out in some shady transaction. Shortly before he really had to be interrupted, he added that army life provided exactly the kind of concentrated boredom he desired; and the combination of boredom and almost total idleness, plus the opportunity to earn money and hang around for a nice fat severance allowance, suited him to a T; he had calculated that – apart from his pay, clothing, board, accommodation, leave, etc. – by 'just being there' he was earning ten marks extra a day, his severance allowance. He even had reason to hope, Kuttke said, that in time certain moral reservations about him (connected with the cause of his demotion) would be dropped, and he would be able as originally planned to enter upon an officer's career with its attendant promotions; and since he intended to get married one day and would certainly 'not forgo the blessing of children', it would appear that after twelve years in the army he could look forward to being discharged, at the age of thirty-three, as a married captain with two children and thus entitled to 'cash in on' a severance allowance of close to eighty-one thousand marks. This would mean that the amount accruing daily by his mere presence would be increased to eighteen or nineteen marks, and the severance allowance would represent an income of over five hundred marks a month – and since his father worked in a bank he could be sure of the most favourable investment opportunities. At thirty-three he would still be a young man and able to start a new life with a nice cushion such as could not easily be obtained by sitting out twelve years in any other profession; moreover, he had discovered that boredom and idleness – apart, of course, from certain chemicals – were the best stimulants, aphrodisiacs if you like, and erotic – that was to say, sexual – experiences were very important to him. 'Woman,' declared Kuttke, 'that continent of pleasure,' had not yet been properly explored, or rather, in our Western civilization she had been suppressed, underestimated. Here he was interrupted by Stollfuss, who asked him to comment on what Gruhl, whom he no doubt recognized in the person of the accused, had been like as a fellow soldier. Kuttke turned toward the younger Gruhl, looked at him as if recognizing him for the first time, slapped his forehead with the palm of his hand as if the reason for his presence here had just dawned on him, and exclaimed, 'Of course, good old Georgie!' Turning to the judge, he said Gruhl had been a 'fine pal'; unfortunately he hadn't been very interested in sex topics, probably owing to a 'strict Catholic upbringing', which he, Kuttke, considered absolutely wrong – although his own strictly Protestant upbringing had been no better, a good measure of hypocrisy being inevitable there too, but... Here it was again necessary to intervene, more sharply than ever, and instruct him severely to keep to the point; oh well, said Kuttke, he could only repeat that Gruhl had been a good pal, but he had taken this whole thing much too seriously and had 'suffered' emotionally from it.

When asked what he meant by 'the whole thing', Kuttke, earning a rebuke for his pun, said: 'the armed farces'. It was ridiculous to speak of 'suffering' in this connection, but Gruhl had *suffered* from this 'quaternity of the absurd' – pointlessness, unproductiveness, boredom, laziness – while he, Kuttke, actually considered these to be the *sole* aim and object of any army. Here Stollfuss lost his temper; raising his voice, he instructed the witness to come to the point and spare the court his private philosophy, Kuttke at once brought his heels smartly together with an abruptness which, although not exaggerated – it could not have been taken for impertinence – was enough to startle those present; with an entirely altered voice he concluded his statement in terse, staccato phrases: 'Fine pal. Dependable. Game for anything. Fetched coffee rations, shared bread and butter, shared sausage: always unselfish, a real pal. Suffered from sense of pointless existence, which he needn't have, since the sum of zero plus zero plus zero is always zero.'

The defence attorney, both the accused, and Aussem (who at a sign from the judge did not take down Kuttke's remarks) listened to Kuttke with deep interest, almost with bated breath. Bergnolte, seated behind the defence attorney and the accused so that he could only be seen by Stollfuss, Kugl-Egger, and Aussem, first gave a sign and then waved his hands in an effort to persuade Stollfuss to break off the hearing; but Stollfuss ignored this just as he did the district attorney's pencil-tapping, which finally became loud enough to embarrass everyone in the room. At last Kugl-Egger, by clearing his throat with a sound that seemed closer to an obscenity, succeeded in bringing Kuttke's mutterings to a halt and interposed a question in the mildest of tones: had he, the witness, ever been ill, mentally ill, that was? Kuttke turned toward him and, with an expression described confidentially by Aussem that evening as 'impassive', said that he was in a permanent state of mental illness; what was more, the district attorney was also in a permanent state of mental illness (the rebuke for this insinuation came promptly, without the district attorney's having to ask for it), and he, Kuttke, made so bold as to put forward the hypothesis that his

'former comrade' Gruhl was not mentally ill, and this was what
had made him 'suffer' so much. There was one thing, though,
and he wanted to emphasize this fact which had been confirmed
by various doctors, specialists and otherwise: he, Kuttke, was
certainly not mentally incompetent; this was of great importance to him, since he had already applied for a licence for his
betting office; no, indeed, the difference between ... But at this
point Stollfuss took pity on poor Bergnolte, who had meanwhile
resorted to wringing his hands in despair, and interrupted
Kuttke to say he had no further questions. Hermes now asked
Kuttke about the reasons for the jeep trip, the end of which was
the subject of these proceedings, and Kuttke became remarkably
business-like. He had put Gruhl 'in the way of' this trip because
he liked him. He was in charge, so to speak – this was one of the
official duties of a staff corporal – of the motor-vehicle records
in the car pool, as well as being responsible for seeing that the
vehicles were always ready for use at a moment's notice, as his
superior, Sergeant Behlau, would be able to confirm. Among
other things it was his job to see that the vehicles were always
ready for inspection; in other words, when inspection-time
came round their speedometers had to show the required mileage. This meant, however, said Kuttke, addressing the defence
attorney in a cool, quiet, well-articulated voice, that there were
sometimes discrepancies. Some vehicles were delivered later
than expected, whereas inspections were carried out as originally
planned; so, in order not to miss the inspection date, which
would mean a further delay, it sometimes happened that vehicles
'had to be raced along the highways to rack up the mileage'. Did
the court, he wondered, realize what he meant: by means of an
unexpectedly elegant twist to his torso, he directed this question
to Stollfuss, Kugl-Egger, and Hermes simultaneously. The three
men looked questioningly at one another, and Stollfuss, who
confessed to knowing nothing about cars, shrugged his shoulders. Well, said Kuttke, whose sigh could have been described as
one of pity, he would explain it by the following example:
supposing a motor vehicle showed a mileage of one thousand
miles but was due for a three-thousand-mile check-up in less

than a week; 'in that case,' he said 'someone has to take off with the car and see that it puts on the required mileage.' Most of these jobs, Kuttke said, he had turned over to Gruhl, who was a very good driver and suffered from boredom because as the carpenter all he had to do was 'polish up fancy furniture for officers' dames and non-coms' squaws'. Stollfuss asked Kuttke whether he would be prepared to repeat what he had just stated under oath, since it was of great importance in judging Gruhl's offence. Kuttke said his statements had been the tooth, the whole tooth, and nothing but the tooth; but before he had to be reprimanded, in fact before this appalling lapse had sunk in properly, he corrected himself and apologized saying it had been a slip of the tongue, for of course he was fully aware of the significance of an oath. What he had meant to say was the truth, the whole truth, and nothing but the truth; he had always, he added with candid, almost childlike chagrin, been apt to mix up words that sounded alike, and had always had a terrible time with the tooth and truth, even had trouble over it in school; but his teacher had been ... At this point he was interrupted by Stollfuss who, without waiting to ask the attorneys for the prosecution and defence, dismissed him. The attorneys both signalled their consent. Kuttke, who waved to Gruhl junior and called out 'Good Luck!' to him as he left, was told to be ready to testify further, Stollfuss announced a half-hour recess, adding that the public was to remain excluded even after the recess.

The flowers had been delivered to Agnes Hall by half-past three. She blushed with pleasure, gave the delivery girl a good tip, and was now reminded for the first time of the hole burned in her new rust-brown silk dress; it was scarcely bigger than a shirt button, and she looked at it with a certain tenderness as she smoothed out the material over her lap; wasn't it also, she thought, a little flower with black edges? Smoking a second cigarillo while drawing up her will, she abandoned herself completely to her emotions; the bequething of all her real and personal property to Gruhl required only a few sentences, but the difficulty lay in phrasing the sole condition: 'annually, on

January 21, St Agnes' Day, to set fire to a jeep belonging to the Bundeswehr, if possible at the place known as "Küpper's Tree", to symbolize a great candle, a fiery sacrament, and in memory of an unknown soldier of the Second World War who was my lover for two days.' Since the Halls, the Hollwegs, and the Schorfs, the whole pack of them, would contest the will, she would presumably have to add a psychiatrist's certificate that she was of sound mind when she had drawn it up. Again and again she crossed out the sentence, added the words 'or its legal successor' behind 'Bundeswehr', gathered up her notes toward half-past-four and, without changing her dress, left the house. She spent some time at the post office, in the flower shop, then at the cemetery at the Hall family grave – an enormous, black-marble monument flanked by larger-than-life bronze angels in noble attitudes – where Stollfuss's parents were also buried. She walked round the church and across the main street to the telephone booth, ordered a taxi which arrived in less than two minutes, and told the driver, a young man who was new to the district, to drive her to 'Küpper's Tree', explaining the best way to get there; the drive took about three minutes, and at 'Küpper's Tree' she got out, asking the driver to wait and turn the taxi around. It was a mild October day, not raining for a change; she looked along the field path, saw the stone on which the Gruhls must have sat, gazed out across the seemingly endless flat sugar-beet fields where harvesting had already begun, went back to the taxi, and was driven to the court-house. The endless flat beet fields with their rich green leaves, the grey-blue sky overhead – the red and black of a fire once a year would bring a little life into this grandiose monotony.

She arrived at the court-house just as Schroer was shutting the public entrance to the courtroom from the inside; looking through the glass pane, he conveyed his regret to her by shaking his head and shrugging his shoulders, and with a quick gesture of his thumb signalled that she should go across to his own apartment. The Schroers and Agnes Hall were on a familiar, almost friendly footing since Fräulein Hall came to the court-house, if not daily, at least three and sometimes four times a week and often, during recess or when the public was not admitted, would sit in the Schroer kitchen chatting with Frau Schroer over a cup of coffee; on this occasion she had first to admire the cake, really an outstanding success. To re-confirm her baking skill, Frau Schroer pierced it once again with a hairpin which, on being drawn out, proved to be immaculate, 'clean as a whistle', as she put it. Frau Schroer also gave a detailed account of old Herr Kirffel's distress and young Herr Kirffel's fainting fit; and the two women, smoking their cigarettes, discussed for a while the question of whether camphor or vinegar water was best in such cases. Frau Schroer took the view that it was a 'matter of type', depending chiefly on the afflicted person's skin : she would, she said, never dare to rub young Herr Kirffel's skin with camphor – he had the skin that goes with red hair although his hair had darkened with age, and it might bring on a rash; whereas she would not hesitate (and she looked at Fräulein Hall with something like approval) to rub Fräulein Hall's skin with camphor ointment. Her eyes fell on the burned hole, it was a shame, she said, and she would be glad when the Gruhls were out of the house; their presence brought too many upheavals – no doubt she knew about the latest complications? When Fräulein Hall said she didn't, she was initiated into the secret of the Schmitz pregnancy; close to tears, Frau Schroer implored Fräulein Hall to exert the whole of her 'not inconsiderable influence' on the Gruhls to prevent its becoming known that it had happened in jail; it could ruin her husband, and Stollfuss too, and she, Frau Schroer, would probably have to face a charge of contributing to immorality, under highly culpable circumstances. Fräulein Hall – laying her hand soothingly on Frau Schroer's arm – promised to talk it over with Hermes, with whom, incidentally, she had something else to discuss. She skilfully brought the conversation back to the topic of 'fainting fits in court' and was amazed at the extensive experience of Frau Schroer, who had red hair, very blue eyes, and an onion-coloured complexion and, on account of her fat legs, was known in Birglar as 'the steam roller'; in an emergency, said Frau Schroer, she was even prepared to give an injection. It was always when the public was excluded that the weirdest things happened, some of them of course nothing but attacks of hysteria, which she cured by a slap in the face; but Dr Hulffen had authorized her and shown her how to give an injection, even an intravenous one, if the necessity arose. When asked how young Herr Kirffel was feeling now, Frau Schroer said he was better but still not equal to going to his office; the two women then discussed the excellent qualities of the Kirffel family, and the integrity of both the Kirffels, father and son. They agreed repeatedly on how 'splendid young Frau Kirffel was', that 'the old man must be very proud to have a nun for a daughter and a monk for a son', and that it would have been a waste, 'a shame, really', for young Kirffel to have entered the Church too. At this point they were interrupted by Schroer, who came in, announced the recess, hung up the keys to the grilles and the cells – a trifle pompously, with something like martial dignity – on a hook over the stove, and poured himself some coffee from the pot; he placed the cup on the table without a saucer and was at once called to order by his wife. She accused him of not being serious enough because he took the Schmitz girl's pregnancy so lightly, and anyway – Frau Schroer's voice now had a hard edge to it – he took everything a bit too lightly, as was plain from the slowness, the snail's pace, of his promotion. Agnes Hall deemed this the right moment to take her departure; she was afraid of Frau Schroer's sharp tongue, for when she was properly worked up she did not hesitate to introduce the most intimate allusions. Fräulein Hall arranged with Schroer that he would telephone her as soon as the public was re-admitted, which, she hoped, would be no later than the pleadings and the verdict. Before leaving the court-house she saw Stollfuss going upstairs with Aussem. She managed to catch Hermes just as he was entering one of the two modern cafés on Birglar's main street. Nervously she realized that she had never been inside either of these cafés before: this one, in which Hermes was looking round for a free table, was huge and even at this hour jammed not with students but with cake-eating farmers' wives who had come in from the country; Fräulein Hall, who never went out, seldom left her house in fact, was amazed to find herself looking at the same heavy physical types that were familiar to her from the dances and church-going days of her youth. She followed Hermes, who took her arm; somewhat flustered, she ordered hot chocolate, taking the drafts of her will out of her handbag as she did so. On edge, because he had planned to avail himself of the recess to compose the first draft of his pleadings, Hermes listened to Fräulein Hall, whom he called 'Auntie', and wondered whether it was the eleventh or even the twelfth time that she had come to him with changes in her will.

Bergnolte decided to go for a short walk, first stepping out rapidly, as he was afraid he would be unable to complete his tour of the 'old centre' of Birglar in half an hour, then more slowly, as he discovered that within twelve minutes he had walked all round and had a good look at the old centre: church, cemetery, the two town gates to east and west, and the medieval town hall, which appeared to house an office of the Bundeswehr; of course, there was also the little bridge over the Duhr, quite attractive with its restored statue of St Nepomuk – a Bohemian saint whom he would not have expected to come across in this part of the country. Black arrows pointing the way to some Roman baths failed to entice him; but, with fifteen minutes still in hand and wishing to avoid any temptation to become embroiled in a conversation with Stollfuss or Kugl-Egger, he succumbed to the lure of the red arrows that promised a 'convent church, 17th cent.'. He found the church at once, entered, and discovered to his astonishment that, although out of practice for twenty years, he went through the motions almost automatically: hand dipped in the stoup, sign of the cross, hint of genuflection toward the altar, a tour of the church 'treading lightly' because he came upon two women praying in front of a Pietà; there were no objects of interest other than an ancient poor-box with wrought-iron mountings, and a modern, bare-looking altar. He strolled slowly – he still had nearly seven minutes left – back to the court-house, once more across the bridge, once more past the statue of St Nepomuk (which, indefinably, seemed to him out of place here); that morning at breakfast his wife had expressed the wish to be transferred to 'a small town, something like this Birglar', and he resolved to oppose her more resolutely than he had yet done. What repelled him particularly was how dirty, 'in fact, unpaved', the streets became as soon as one left the main street 'in the old centre'. To be sure, there were a few handsome old patrician houses; there was also, if he should seriously consider it, the concrete prospect of immediately stepping into Stollfuss's shoes, and yet ... it didn't particularly appeal to him. After paying a quick visit to one of the many notorious court-house toilets he emerged on to the former playground again and almost collided with Lieutenant Heimüller, who was strolling about among the old trees in a mood apparently far from cheerful. Bergnolte introduced himself, saying he was a 'legal expert acting as an observer'; then, shaking his head, he brought up the subject of Kuttke and tried to find out what kind of testimony could be expected from the sergeant. The lieutenant, who saw that Bergnolte's concern was genuine and accepted it gratefully, spoke with a sigh of Private Kuttke's 'many peculiar idiosyncrasies'; he confirmed with a nod that Kuttke was 'quite impossible', and then in the few remaining minutes indulged in his pet theory of an '*élite* of purity', which caused Bergnolte to frown. Heimüller just had time to ask Bergnolte how long he thought it would be before he was called; he was of course, like all soldiers, used to waiting, but ... Bergnolte reassured him that after the recess it would be a matter of barely twenty minutes.

After the recess Stollfuss managed to talk Hermes out of calling Motrik, the art dealer from the city, as a witness. There had already, he said, been abundant evidence of Gruhl's ability, and – he added in a low voice and with a melancholy smile, before entering the courtroom – any 'gleam of hope' that he, Hermes, might have of extending the proceedings beyond one day was quite vain. Arson and sabotage, and Stollfuss, now in the doorway – Hermes's clients wouldn't get away with less than four or five years' penitentiary, and was 'that bit of publicity' really worth so much to Hermes? Hermes agreed resignedly to dispense with Motrik, who had refused to enter the 'stuffy witness room' and was waiting in the corridor. On being told apologetically by Hermes that he had been summoned for nothing, Motrik, a long-haired individual no longer in his first youth, wearing a camel-hair coat and suède gloves, uttered the word 'shit' in a manner indicating that it did not form part of his normal vocabulary. Nor did he succeed, as he went back to his green Citroën, in investing his walk with that 'infinite contempt' which the strong word had been intended to impart. He seemed too much like a man who strives in vain to convey an impression of masterful virility.

Contrary to expectation, the hearing of the two remaining witnesses, Lieutenant Heimüller and Sergeant Behlau, who gave their evidence separately, went smoothly and without so much as a ripple of sensation. Behlau, the first to be called after the recess, entered the courtroom erect and faultlessly neat; he gave his age as twenty-seven, his occupation as soldier, his rank as sergeant, and in precise terms confirmed the facts as already stated by Kuttke: that he, Behlau, was in charge of the car pool, and that Kuttke, his immediate subordinate, was also responsible for the car pool. A lengthy explanation as to the difference between rank and post, which Behlau – in view of the fact that Kuttke was responsible for the car pool although only a private first class – evidently felt was due to the court, was politely cut short by Stollfuss, with the remark that this difference applied also to the civil service. In response to the defence attorney's question, Behlau confirmed the practice of racking up the mileage, which he called 'use of a vehicle for speedometer adjustment', and volunteered the information that Kuttke, although he might have made a 'rather odd impression', as a soldier was beyond criticism; if their unit had an excellent reputation for the care and handling of motor vehicles, and indeed it had often been complimented on this account, no small measure of credit for this was due to Kuttke. This unexpectedly objective attitude of Behlau's was acknowledged by an approving nod from Bergnolte and Aussem. When asked how many times a year a motorized unit had to undertake these 'speedometer adjustments', Behlau replied that it might happen two or three times a year. On being questioned by the district attorney about Gruhl junior, Behlau said that although Gruhl had not been what you might call an enthusiastic soldier – very few were, after all – he had been not so much insubordinate as morose and indifferent; he had gone absent without leave a few times and been duly punished – but then that wasn't a crime, it was practically the normal thing. Behlau, who seemed quite different here from the way he had behaved in the witness room and the way he customarily behaved in bars and taverns, left a very good impression on the court. He was businesslike, dignified, not overbearingly military; he was told to stand ready for further questioning.

After Behlau had left and Lieutenant Heimüller had been called, Dr Hermes expressed a politely worded protest against the exclusion of the public; he pointed out that he was well aware that this measure only affected his wife – who, as a qualified attorney, not only assisted him but was fully informed about all aspects of the case and, needless to say, would respect the need for secrecy – and Huppenach, the young farmer, who knew all about the affair since he had done his military service at the same time and in the same unit as Gruhl. Now – he gestured ironically to the empty spectator chairs – matters were being dealt with that were not so much military as administrative secrets, and that was just the kind of thing that was so interesting to the public; the subject was neither a strategic nor a tactical secret : it merely exposed the absurdity of a wasteful administration. With quiet deliberation, while Heimüller was already standing inside the room waiting discreetly to be called, Stollfuss explained to the defence attorney that the very thing he called the absurdity of a wasteful administration was not suitable for public discussion : the state had the right – and he, Stollfuss was exerting this right at the request of the attorney for the prosecution – not to permit the public at large to examine this unavoidable wastefulness which, after all, represented not so much the intrinsic objective of the operation as an inevitable concomitant. In any case, he could not accede to the defence attorney's request to re-admit the public. He then asked Lieutenant Heimüller to step forward, apologizing for the delay that had ensued after he had already been called.

Heimüller gave his age as twenty-three, his occupation as soldier, and his rank as first lieutenant in the communications branch; he also volunteered the fact that he was a Roman Catholic. This additional fact, uttered in firm tones, gave rise to some embarrassment among the lawyers present; they exchanged glances, there was a brief whispering between Aussem and the judge, and the latter instructed Aussem to strike this additional item from the record. Aussem reported that evening that Heimüller's voice in proclaiming his religion had sounded like a 'clarion call'. Heimüller, who during his testimony frequently turned – as if solicitously – toward young Gruhl, confirmed substantially what Behlau had said regarding Gruhl's qualities as a soldier, only he expressed himself differently. He described him as being 'unquestionably gifted', and when asked by the defence attorney to define the field in which he was gifted, Heimüller said 'as a soldier'. This made Gruhl junior laugh and, although it did not prompt a reprimand, it led to an involved explanation on the part of the lieutenant, who reminded him how he, Gruhl, had helped him during manoeuvres in the working out and plotting of deployment areas. Thereupon Gruhl, whom it then really became necessary to reprimand, joined, uninvited, in Heimüller's testimony and expressed the opinion that those had been childish abstract games with their own particular, even artistic, appeal. After all, and this was his philosophy, the function of art was to classify nothing into its various nothingness, and the establishing and plotting of deployment areas had a certain undeniable graphic attraction. Stollfuss noticed that it was not yet seven and that the proceeding would be wound up by eight at the latest; he was rather proud of the fact that, despite all the unforeseen and sometimes unwelcome digressions, the trial had been conducted as he had planned it, so he listened quite patiently to young Gruhl and

133

did not interrupt him until he had almost finished. The lieutenant continued with his assessment of young Gruhl, describing him as 'intelligent, not insubordinate, but almost shamefully indifferent'; generally speaking he had behaved quite well, although on a few occasions – 'or, I should say, actually quite often: to be precise, five times' – he had exceeded his leave, 'and on three occasions quite considerably', and had been punished. When asked by the defence attorney whether on the day of the 'incident' Gruhl had been a soldier or a civilian, Heimüller replied that 'at the time of the incident' Gruhl had been *de facto* a soldier but *de jure* a civilian; the Bundeswehr – he had reconfirmed this with his superior – was not appearing here as a co-plaintiff and did not intend to prosecute Gruhl under military law. It had been discovered only after the event that, due to unavoidable errors in the records, Gruhl, who was due to discharge around this time, should have had a visit to his father (who was suffering from severe bronchitis) booked as four days' compassionate leave, whereas those four days had been erroneously entered as part of his normal leave; hence 'at the time of the incident' Gruhl had already been *de facto* a civilian. The defence attorney asked if any consideration were being given to laying a charge, even as a formality, against Gruhl for unauthorized wearing of a uniform and unauthorized driving of a Bundeswehr jeep, since *de jure* Gruhl was guilty of these offences, and a clarification of the legal aspect required at least the formality of such proceedings? The defence attorney's irony escaped the lieutenant; earnest and conscientious, he replied at some length that Gruhl was not guilty of these two offences – although he had indeed committed them – or at least, was not guilty by his own volition; personally he did not know of any such proceedings being under consideration. Then, in response to the defence attorney's questions, to which Kuttke and Behlau had given essentially the same answers, concerning these sinister trips, this 'racking up of mileage', Heimüller confirmed both Kuttke's and Behlau's statements: yes, he said, these did occur, for it was a much greater nuisance to postpone the inspection when it was due than to rack up the 'mileage required by the inspection'. The defence attorney: It could be argued whether the term 'due' as applying to such an inspection was permissible; he drove a car himself, and an inspection was only due when the speedometer had reached the required figure in the natural way, in other words, through normal official usage; if he might be permitted to say so, this method seemed to him 'utterly senseless'. The district attorney protested against the introduction of philosophical and extraneous aspects and at the hairsplitting over a word like 'due': in an institution such as the Bundeswehr, consideration must be given to mobility and preparedness; and what might appear senseless – something which an outsider was not entitled to judge – might often be the more sensible method. Similar instances occurred in every institution – even 'the law'. On being asked for details of this particular trip, Heimüller replied, yes, Kuttke and Behlau had suggested Gruhl to him and he had sent Gruhl off on a five-day test run, alone; although this was not *quite* according to regulations, it was not only tolerated but even permitted. Gruhl had only driven, as was later ascertained, from Düren to Limburg on the autobahn, then from the autobahn down to the Rhine and along the Rhine toward his home, where he had arrived at his father's just before six in the evening; there he had remained until the alleged offence had been committed. The district attorney asked Gruhl junior to comment on the recorded statements of Frau Leuffen, his grandmother, and Frau Wermelskirchen, their neighbour, which confirmed that he had driven the jeep into an empty barn, had left it there for four days, and during the period in question had lived at home and worked with his father. Gruhl confirmed these statements in every detail, as did his father; when asked by the defence attorney whether Gruhl had not violated the regulations by this deviation from the prescribed mission, Heimüller said that although such deviations did constitute violations, they were tolerated; moveover, Gruhl had merely been instructed to bring the speedometer up to the required reading and had been free – if not explicitly then certainly by implication – to choose his own route; it was a fact that, as police investigation of the wreck had revealed, the speedometer had read 2,994 miles. Gruhl had arrived at this figure by blocking up the jeep and letting the motor idle, and had used a tube to draw off the fumes into the open; the sound of the running motor, in spite of certain acoustical changes created by bales of straw and hay, had also been confirmed by both Frau Leuffen and Frau Wermelskirchen. The judge accounted for the fact that these details were only now coming to light by explaining that they came under the heading of official secrets. The idea of blocking up the jeep had originated with Gruhl senior: during the construction of the so-called West Wall in 1938–9 he had seen this done and sometimes taken a hand; the method was an old trick of fraudulent cartage companies, which used it to cheat on mileage tariffs. All this was also confirmed by Gruhl father and son, the latter stating that the figure 2,994 had been deliberately arrived at. It was an element of his artistic composition; the significance of this last term would become clear from the defence attorney's pleadings. Asked about the credibility and character of Private Kuttke, the lieutenant said that, hard though it might be to believe, Kuttke was extremely serious, almost pernickety, about his job; the lieutenant's unit had frequently been complimented on the excellent condition of its vehicles, and the credit belonged to Kuttke; as to the personal angle – well, the court had probably taken note of Kuttke's personal idiosyncrasies. The way Heimüller shrugged his shoulders betokened not so much resignation as sincere regret, and he went on to say that he could envision a different procedure for selecting professional soldiers; but Kuttke was legally, or he should say in the eyes of the law, a soldier, and there were no two ways about it. He himself had dreams of an army of purity, of uprightness – but this was no doubt not the place to expound his personal philosophy concerning the armed forces. The judge nodded in agreement and looked questioningly at the two attorneys, who both signalled that they had no further need of Lieutenant Heimüller. The judge thanked the young officer and asked him kindly to tell his subordinates that they were also excused.

*

Stollfuss called Kugl-Egger and Hermes over for a short consultation and did not even lower his voice when he asked them whether they would prefer to have a short recess *now*, or to start with the hearing of Professor Büren and *then* have a longer recess, of thirty or forty minutes, before beginning the last act, which would consist of final hearings of the accused, the pleadings, and the verdict. Hermes pointed out that Büren's evidence would probably take some time, whereas Kugl-Egger irritably declared the testimony of an art expert to be superfluous. After a brief consultation with his clients (Gruhl senior said they would be having a cold supper anyway and the red wine wouldn't spoil either), Hermes consented to begin right away with Büren's evidence. Stollfuss now called Schroer over and asked him whether his wife could manage, as she had so often done in similar circumstances, to provide some refreshments in the way of a snack and something to drink. Schroer replied that his wife had already sensed that a 'marathon' was on the agenda for today, and was prepared to provide coffee at any time; ample supplies of beer were also on hand, 'wieners, too, and of course sandwiches, bouillon, and potato salad, and, if I'm not mistaken, some beef stew (canned, I'm afraid) and hard-boiled eggs'. He asked Stollfuss, who had nodded at this reassuring information, whether he might open the door and re-admit the public. Was anyone still waiting, Stollfuss asked; yes, said Schroer, Fräulein Hall was 'most interested in the further course of the proceedings'. Neither Kugl-Egger nor Hermes had any objection to the door being opened; in fact Bergnolte now gave the first indication that his presence was not quite without its official aspect and also nodded his consent. Schroer went to the door and unlocked it; Agnes Hall walked in and sat down unobtrusively in the last of the four rows of chairs. She had changed her clothes and was wearing a dark-green tweed skirt and a loose jacket of a slightly paler green, the cuffs and collar edged with narrow bands of chinchilla. There was some discussion later on as to whether Stollfuss had nodded to her or whether the movement of his head described as a nod had merely meant he was 'immersing himself' in his documents. In

Aussem's view, there was something of both in this movement: for an immersing of himself in his documents it had not been mechanical or automatic enough, yet for a nod it had been too slight; in any case, he was sure of one thing, he had seen Stollfuss immerse himself in documents often enough and it had certainly been more than that. Schroer said afterwards that it had been *only* a nod, and that he was familiar with the way Stollfuss moved his head; whereas Hermes declared that 'there was absolutely no question of its being even remotely a nod'. The only other person interested in this movement of the judge's head, Agnes Hall herself, was in no doubt whatever that it had been a nod, and in her own mind she even registered it as 'friendly'.

The appearance of Professor Büren as a witness in the dimly lit courtroom would have merited not only a larger but a considerable audience; one detail in the description of Büren's manner subsequently gave rise to a controversy between Aussem, with his strong literary leanings, and Hermes, who was less interested in such nuances. Hermes objected to Aussem's description of Büren's manner as 'crisply casual', saying that the concept of 'casualness' precluded any element of 'crispness'; Aussem countered by saying that, on the contrary, casualness had need of crispness and crispness of casualness, as witness the term 'dashing' – dashing comprised both casualness and crispness, and the reason he did not describe Büren's manner as dashing was because he found the term hackneyed, so he would stick to his original description: that Büren's manner had been one of crisp casualness. It was obvious that, upon a professor's being called as a witness, none of those present – except Hermes, who had already met Büren several times in connection with this action – expected to be faced with anyone looking like Büren; for the first time even the Gruhls showed some curiosity. Büren was wearing a very loose mustard-coloured corduroy jacket; and because Hermes had told him it would probably be better to appear wearing a tie, he wore, in addition to his mustard-coloured shirt, a rather thick gold cord knotted round his neck, the kind of cord used to tie Christmas presents; his trousers were spinach green and his shoes were made of very loosely woven strips of leather, hardly more than sandals. By contrast he wore his hair cut in a perfectly conventional manner; moreover, he was well-shaven and beardless; his tanned, healthy face – 'such nice eyes, like a spaniel's' as Agnes Hall later called them – beamed benignly as he supplied the following facts about himself in a hoarse voice: thirty-four years old, married, seven children, not related to the accused either by blood or marriage. In response to a brief request by Hermes, he stated that he had examined the 'incident', the subject of these proceedings, very minutely, had read all the relevant statements including the one that was of most importance to him, that of Erbel the travelling salesman, and he had just been told by Herr Hermes that the vital details supplied by Erbel had been corroborated by a police officer during the course of today's proceedings; some highly interesting points had been described in this statement, and might he ask the two accused men a question? On receiving the judge's consent, Büren, whose face never lost its benign expression, asked young Gruhl how he had managed to produce that musical sound which had been described by some as explosive, by others as a kind of drumming, and by Erbel as 'beautiful, in a way'. Gruhl junior, after conferring in a whisper with Hermes, got up and said he could not divulge the secret because it was one of the few elements of his style that he intended to develop. He was planning more of this kind of thing; he had already been to a scrap heap and looked round for empty drums or tanks 'the size of locomotives', so that, as soon as he had the time and the opportunity, he could give a concert. The event now under consideration and which had caused him to be charged with property damage had been nothing but a 'preliminary experiment, although a successful one', which he intended to carry on. When told by Stollfuss that he should have confidence in the discretion of all those present, including Fräulein Hall, and should not withhold this information from the professor, Gruhl said he was sure the 'witness Büren' had plagiaristic intentions like most artists; even then Büren's cheerfulness remained undiminished, and he admitted that his curiosity was not altogether altruistic but pointed out that he, Büren, belonged to an entirely different branch of art and gave his solemn promise not to betray the secret outside the courtroom. Gruhl junior again conferred with his attorney, and the latter requested the judge to see that Gruhl's statement was entered in the record 'so as to establish a kind of copyright'. Stollfuss, who was in the best of spirits, instructed Aussem to record Gruhl's statement. Gruhl junior, whose suspicions had now yielded to the generally pervading good humour, informed the court that he had produced these sounds partly with malt candies and partly with cream caramels: in other words, the more sombre tones with the malt candies, the lighter ones with the cream caramels. He had first emptied the two gasoline cans into the jeep, then punctured them full of holes, and, after filling them with malt candies and cream caramels, screwed the tops on again; the fire, the blaze, had produced the desired effect. Earlier experiments with lemon drops and what were known as satin cushions, in which he had used a large tin can, had failed because the stuff had melted and dissolved into a pulpy mass instead of 'making music'; he had also experimented with goat droppings and broken sticks of barley sugar – no luck. The district attorney, who was beginning to lose his temper as well as his patience because, as he later admitted, he 'was beginning to regret having allowed those cunning Rhineland devils to saddle him with this trial', now asked Büren whether he was a *full* professor or an assistant professor. Büren, unable to restrain a giggle, said he was neither one nor the other but a professor at the Art Academy in the city, and his order of investiture had been signed by the premier himself; he must admit he didn't always carry this document with him or on him, but it was certainly 'to be found somewhere at home'; he was even entitled to a pension, and furthermore – another giggle – although he had been 'passed over' during the last election of directors, he was sure that next time he 'would stand a pretty good chance'. His sculptures, he added, were to be found in, 'wait a moment', he said and counted on his fingers, under his breath, up to seven, 'in seven museums, three of them abroad. There's no doubt about my being a civil servant, you know,' he said to the district attorney, still beaming. The district attorney, making no attempt to suppress his annoyance, now asked the judge whether he could be told, or whether his esteemed colleague Hermes might be good enough to tell him, why Professor Büren had been asked to testify. Hermes: the professor was there to deomonstrate that the 'alleged offence' – he managed to convey the quotation marks – which had already been referred to as the 'incident', had been a work of art. The moment Kugl-Egger saw Stollfuss nodding in response to this and saw that Bergnolte – at whom Kugl-Egger was gazing imploringly, his hands raised in mute appeal – was avoiding the issue by lowering his eyes and making imaginary entries in his notebook, he knew, as he told his wife later, 'that I had been sold down the river'.

When asked by Hermes to define this new art trend or, should he say, art form now known internationally as a Happening, Büren said he wished to emphasize that he espoused the fine old tradition of non-representational sculpture and expressed himself in that art form; he had received – here he addressed himself pointedly, although with kindly irony, to the district attorney – two national awards; in other words: *he* was not a Happening-man, but he had taken a deep interest in and had carefully explored this art which called itself anti-art. It was an attempt, if he understood it correctly – and who did, when it came to that? – to create a liberating disorder, not form but non-form, non-beauty in fact; but its direction was determined by the artist, or performer, creating new form out of non-form. In this sense, the incident in question was 'without the slightest doubt a work of art'; it was in fact a most remarkable performance since it incorporated five dimensions: those of architecture, sculpture, literature, music – for it had certainly included musical aspects – and finally elements of the dance, expressed, in his view, by the men knocking their pipes together. There was only one thing – and here Büren frowned disapprovingly – that had bothered him: the expression 'warming up' as used by one of the accused. This was a definite, if minor, limitation of the event's artistic character, for one could not maintain that a work of art existed for purposes of providing warmth; he was also critical of the fact that a new, almost brand-new, vehicle had been used, although he fully realized that it had to be a motor vehicle, and a usable one at that. Gasoline, motor vehicle, fire, explosion – there was no doubt that elements of modern technology had been combined here into a composition of well-nigh inspired artistry. At this point the district attorney, his subsiding rage now replaced by a resignation shot through with malice, asked the witness whether his testimony was to be taken as factual or relatively objective, whereupon Büren replied with a smile that 'factual' and 'relatively objective' were terms of art criticism which were not applicable to such a work of art as this. Wouldn't it then, asked the district attorney, have been possible to choose a different instrument, why did it have to be a jeep; this brought an ominous smile from Büren. Every artist chose his material himself; no one could interfere or suggest here, and if an artist believed that it had to be a *new* jeep, then a new jeep it had to be. Was it, asked the district attorney, whose profound bitterness now sounded almost optimistic again, was it then customary for an artist seeking material for a work of art to – he uttered the word with unconcealed scorn – steal it? Büren countered with that crisp casualness which Aussem later described as fantastic: he said that the desire to create a work of art was a passion of such intensity that an artist would be absolutely prepared at any time to steal his material; Picasso, he went on, had often picked up material for his creations from garbage dumps, and on one occasion even the Bundeswehr had allowed some jet-fighter engines to participate for a few minutes in a creation of this kind. He did not have much more to say, but one thing was certain: the event had constituted the creation of a work of art of a high order; it had involved, as he had said, not only the five dimensions but the five Muses. Of course, the ultimate aim was to unite the nine Muses, but to combine five Muses in one creation, that was 'pretty good'; since religious literature in the form of a litany had formed part of the performance he had but little hesitation in going so far as to describe this work of art as Christian, seeing that saints had been appealed to. Would it be possible, Büren now asked with disarming modesty, for him to leave now; he had – he found it very embarrassing, 'horribly embarrassing' in fact, to have to mention it, but he had an appointment with the premier and, although he had told him he was being delayed in a matter of the utmost importance, he ought not perhaps to keep this gentleman waiting *too* long. The district attorney said he had no further questions and would abstain from certain comments which he would like to make; but he reserved the right to call a further expert, since he regarded Büren not as a witness but as an expert. Hermes asked leave to put just one more question and explained briefly to Büren that Erbel, the travelling salesman, had been asked by the younger Gruhl for a sample of the bath oil he was selling; his client had confessed to him that he had required the bath oil as an additional component for his creation. His question to the witness was whether a 'fair amount' of this bath oil, which was known to produce yellowish-green or blue foam, did not represent the additional element of painting; that was to say, whether it would not have introduced a sixth dimension or a sixth Muse? Büren confirmed this, saying that the notion of adding bath oil was an ingenious variation of the effects. Having received the judge's thanks and permission to leave, he was now free to keep his appointment with the premier.

Four

Büren's departure was followed by an uproar which Aussem was not allowed to enter in the record. Throwing all restraint to the winds and addressing neither Stollfuss nor Bergnolte directly, the district attorney shouted at the top of his voice that he reserved the right to withdraw from the case; he felt he had been 'double-crossed', not so much by his colleague Hermes, who had every right to manoeuvre his clients into the most favourable position, but – here he raised his hands in a gesture of supplication, as if calling on God or at least the Goddess of Justice for aid – 'elsewhere, at a higher level, I have allowed myself to be jockeyed into a position which compels me to a course of irresponsibility foreign to my nature. I withdraw from the case!' Kugl-Egger, still youthful but of considerable corpulence, clutched at his heart in a flash of fear; the movement prompted Schroer to spring to his side, calling out to Gruhl senior, 'Quick, Johann, go and get Lisa!' thereby committing a double breach of regulations: not only had he addressed a prisoner by his first name but he had dispatched him from the courtroom without due cause. Kugl-Egger, almost inert, allowed himself to be led by Schroer into the kitchen; his purplish face, the face of a man who likes his food and won't say no to a glass of beer, did not even register disapproval when young Gruhl, without waiting to be asked, ran forward to help Schroer and – contrary to regulations, like his father – left the courtroom to assist Kugl-Egger into the Schroers' kitchen. Frau Schroer was already waiting with her trusty camphor ointment (she had instinctively diagnosed the district attorney's dermatological disposition correctly; Frau Schroer later to Agnes Hall: 'That man has a hide like a horse!'); she firmly unbuttoned his jacket and vest, pushed up his shirt, and massaged 'the heart region' with her fine strong hands.

Meanwhile Bergnolte had darted across to Stollfuss (who forgot to declare a recess) and accompanied him upstairs to the judge's chambers; he already had his hand on the telephone receiver when Stollfuss pointed out that, regardless of Kugl-Egger's emotional and physical state, it would nevertheless be advisable to consult him before alerting Grellber. Bergnolte, whose face now wore a look that could safely have been described as 'sheer panic', asked Stollfuss in a whisper – although no whisper was necessary, since there was not the slightest chance of being overheard – whether they mightn't ask Herr Hermann, another district attorney, to jump into the breach, since he was known to be spending his vacation right here in Birglar. Stollfuss, who had lighted a cigarette, far from showing any sign of being upset by this untoward incident, seemed almost to be enjoying it; he pointed out to Bergnolte that *such* a precipitate move might alert the press. Bergnolte, unsteadily lighting a cigarette, said – still in a whisper – this business *had* to be 'got out of the way today, even it it takes till three in the morning'. He left Stollfuss to himself, and the judge took the opportunity to telephone his wife and say he probably wouldn't be home before midnight but she wasn't to worry. His wife told him that Grellber had phoned again and informed her, with his usual charm, that Stollfuss might expect to receive a decoration, probably a very high one. In the meantime Kugl-Egger, thanks not only to the strong, fine hands of Frau Schroer but also to brandy skilfully poured between his lips by Gruhl senior, was sufficiently restored to be able to mount the stairs and carry on a lengthy telephone conversation in his office.

In the courtroom Hermes was chatting with Agnes Hall, young Aussem, and Gruhl junior – now returned from the Schroer kitchen – about Gruhl's impending wedding to the lovely Eva. Gruhl junior also announced his intention of going into business for himself, taking over his father's workshop, and employing his father 'at a wage below the attachable minimum'.

Agnes Hall, who now told him in the presence of his attorney that she was willing to pay for all the damage, received a kiss from him and was invited to the wedding, along with Hermes and Aussem. Gruhl was still on first-name terms with the latter, dating from the time when they had both been members of a football club known as the 'Birglar Eagles', in which Gruhl had played fullback and Aussem left halfback. Aussem then explained to the others how much he deplored the fate which obliged him, as court recorder, to observe the rules of secrecy, and went on to say that young Gruhl would have done better to use a dodge or two to get out of his military service – there were very simple ways of doing this.

In the Schroer kitchen, while Gruhl senior and Schroer were using this respite 'to have a quick one', they were informed by an agitated Frau Schroer that it was not Eva who had taken the cold supper over to the Gruhls but her father, Schmitz himself, who in none too cordial terms had expressed his opinion of the 'wrong done to his daughter' and was threatening to sue the court authorities for contributing to immorality; just *how* far from cordial his reactions were was apparent from the quality of the supper, which consisted of sandwiches spread with margarine and coarse liver sausage, and a bottle of soda water. The men laughed at Frau Schroer's anxiety, saying they knew how to deal with Schmitz; no father or mother could be expected to take 'such things' lightly; it was only natural for them to be upset; besides, it could be proved that 'it' had happened after old Herr Leuffen's funeral and not within these walls. She needn't get excited for Schmitz had no reason in the world 'to act the upstanding, law-abiding citizen'. The only one who would really suffer was his wife, Gertrud; she certainly deserved an explanation, an apology in fact, but Pitter had a thick hide and could come and take back his margarine sandwiches tomorrow. At this point Schroer was interrupted by Bergnolte, with a message from Stollfuss that a half-hour recess had been called, and His Honour would like a snack taken to him upstairs – a cup of bouillon, a hard-boiled egg, and some potato salad. This prompted Frau Schroer to remark that eggs, especially hard-boiled ones, were 'not good' for men over fifty; as she did so she gave Bergnolte a searching look, apparently satisfying herself that he was of an age at which he 'might just' be able to eat hard-boiled eggs without coming to any harm. Bergnolte, who – as he told Grellber late that same night – found 'the whole atmosphere really very peculiar', then asked for a hard-boiled egg, a cup of bouillon, and a slice of bread and butter. He was shown into the Schroers' living room, where the table had been set for him, Fräulein Hall, young Aussem, and Hermes. The two Gruhls were duly led back to their cells; in Schroer's walk, in that perhaps faintly underlined martial tread of the sheriff's officer, in the rattle of his bunch of keys, Bergnolte thought he detected 'the kind of corruption against which we are struggling in vain, Herr President'. In Bergnolte's presence the three remaining persons, Hermes, Fräulein Hall, and Aussem, seemed for a time to have been deserted by their Rhineland volubility; and in the case of Hermes, an optimistic young man who loved a good chat, this struck a strangely unnatural note. Finally he did blurt out a question to his Aunt Hall and asked her about her turkeys: were they doing as well this year as in previous years, and would she again be donating two choice specimens for the raffle at the Catholic Academic ball? Aussem now joined in and begged her with mock humility 'please not to forget the Liberals either', they were holding their dance on St Barbara's Day, whereupon Agnes Hall said that if she were asked she would even give the Communists two choice specimens – should they be holding a ball on, say, St Thomas's Day. This little joke, which finally relaxed the tension around the rather small table in the Schroer's living room, was greeted with spontaneous laughter in which Bergnolte joined rather sourly; he later referred to this joke as 'carrying things a bit too far'.

Meanwhile Frau Schroer toasted a slice of white bread for Kugl-Egger in the kitchen and made him an omelette, 'as light as a feather'; she advised her husband not to give him any beer, or any bouillon either, saying she thought it would be wiser to take him a glass of water with 'a generous dash of brandy' in it.

Had Aussem been authorized to enter in his official records the mood in which the proceedings were resumed and concluded, the only adjective he could have used to define it would have been 'subdued', or perhaps even 'fatigued'. Kugl-Egger, in particular, seemed unnaturally meek. In response to a sign from Stollfuss, he rose to his feet and said in an unusually soft, almost humble voice that he withdrew what he had said before the recess and admitted to having succumbed to a mood unworthy of a professional man in his position – although it had perhaps been understandable. With the consent of His Honour the judge, he would resume his duties and once again take full responsibility for them. Everyone in the room, even Bergnolte, felt touched by his humility, and this atmosphere set the tone for the further course of the proceedings. The two accused men, whom Stollfuss now instructed to give their final explanation, were noticeably considerate. Gruhl senior, the first to speak, even directed his statement exclusively to the district attorney, so much so that Stollfuss was obliged to indicate by a fatherly nod and an appropriate gesture that remarks must be addressed to himself, the judge. The accused said that, in order not to leave any of the ladies and gentlemen present under a misapprehension, he must repeat what he had said at the beginning: he was totally indifferent to the law; his reasons for testifying had been purely personal, because 'this business' involved so many people whom he knew personally and for whom he had a great regard. As to the affair itself, all he had to say was this: he was not an artist, nor did he have any artistic ambitions; while he could appreciate art, he was incapable of creating anything himself, but he had discovered that his son was gifted and had agreed to take part in the affair. In the true sense of the word he was a participant; but the word participant applied only to his share in the subsequent work of art, not to his share in the offence, assuming there had been any offence. His was the greater responsibility in the offence, for he was the older; besides, it was *he* who had introduced the financial element by explaining to his son, who had discussed the plan and it's 'dramatic sequence' in detail with him. The value of such a vehicle corresponded to

148

less than a quarter of the sum he had paid in taxes over the last few years, and to only a fifth of what he still owed; furthermore, so he had told his son, they could deduct the cost from income tax as art material, just as a painter could deduct canvas, paint, and frames. He therefore acknowledged his guilt to the extent that he had 'encouraged' his son to 'borrow from the Bundeswehr on this admittedly somewhat arbitrary basis'. In view of his attitude toward the law, he requested the court to appreciate why he was not asking for either an acquittal or a fair sentence, but was awaiting 'whatever was in store for him, like rain or sunshine'. Neither defence nor prosecution had any further questions to put to him.

Gruhl junior also remained unruffled and polite, but in a way which Agnes Hall later held against him as 'inclined to be stuck-up'. He said his own lack of concern differed from his father's; his related more to the value of the jeep. He had been sent on this kind of mission, the nature of which had already been adequately described and documented, a total of four times in one year and had thus 'racked up some twelve thousand miles, equivalent to half way around the world'. He had been obliged to 'squander' more than eight hundred gallons of gasoline and a corresponding amount of oil – mostly by 'driving up and down' the autobahn between Düren and Frankfurt; moreover, he had witnessed senseless waste in time, material, energy, and patience in other areas of the military system. And finally, merely in order to rack up those twelve thousand miles, he had been on the road for more than twenty-five days, 'for the sole purpose of keeping the speedometer in motion'. As a carpenter he had been put to jobs that he had found 'downright repulsive'; for months he had worked at setting up bars, first for an officers' mess, then for a non-coms' mess, and what it boiled down to was a 'badly paid imposition'. He was interrupted here by Stollfuss, who told him firmly that this was not the time or place to volunteer his philosophy of military service and he must keep to the point. Young Gruhl apologized and resumed his statement, saying he was an artist, and a work of art for which government or official approval had to be obtained, as had been the case with all Hap-

penings so far, was in his eyes not a work of art. The obtaining of
material and the location of a site were the risks every artist ran;
he had planned this event and got hold of the material. He
would just like to emphasize: *he* had paid for the gasoline,
about twenty gallons, out of his own pocket since he 'couldn't
be bothered' to drive to the barracks and fill up, as he was
entitled to do, at the army filling station. He did admit one
thing, though: the 'object', a jeep, had possibly been too large;
he might have achieved the desired effect with something
smaller. He was now contemplating using gasoline cans only,
and building a pyramid of rifles in the middle of them – he had
asked a friend, a go-between, to make some inquiries about rifles;
these would then be set fire to, using the 'candy explosion'
method, and allowed to burn down until the remaining metal
parts could be welded together into a sculpture. He was again
cut short by Stollfuss, who told him all this was irrelevant and
asked young Gruhl whether he realized something his father obviously had realized: that the appropriation of such costly
material constituted a violation of the law. Yes, said Gruhl
junior, he realized that; but – he supposed it was all right to
announce this now – the loss was going to be made good, at
once if necessary, and needless to say he would in future create
only works of art for which the material would be provided,
obtained, and paid for by himself.

Since neither defence nor prosecution had any more questions
to put to Gruhl junior, Kugl-Egger was asked to commence his
pleadings; he declined the offer of a short preparatory pause,
got to his feet, put on his biretta, and began to speak. Kugl-
Egger had recovered not only his self-control but his poise; he
spoke in a calm, unhurried voice and without notes, looking
neither at the accused nor at the judge but beyond the judge's
head at a spot on the wall that had been intriguing him all day.
There on the faded old paint (described at regular intervals in
the appropriate renovation requests as being in 'shocking condition') it was just possible, if one looked hard enough, to make
out the place where a crucifix had once hung in the days when
the building still served as a school; in fact, as Kugl-Egger later

claimed, you could even see 'the mark, running diagonally up to the right, almost like a railway signal, which must have been left by the boxwood twig'. Kugl-Egger spoke in a low voice, his tone mild without being exactly humble; Gruhl senior had been glorified as an 'expert in great demand', and his financial position greatly overemphasized, by the defence in the attempt to depict his career as that of a true martyr of human society; moreover, the procession of defence witnesses had left him with an impression exactly contrary to the one that had been desired: a man who was basically such a fine person must, in his opinion at least, be held much more strictly to his responsibilities than someone of lesser merit. His own reaction had been the same as Inspector Kirffel's: the bare-faced confession horrified him. He considered that the charges had been entirely substantiated: property damage and public mischief. Both charges had been not only fully proven but admitted. Furthermore, the wastefulness in the Bundeswehr had been overemphasized; this wastefulness applied to every field of daily and economic life. In the meantime, still staring at the impression of the crucifix, he had discovered, as he told his wife later that evening, a number of boxwood traces; this made him smile in a manner that was misinterpreted by all those present. With this gentle, rather beautiful smile on his face he went on to say that there had been much talk here of art, of form and non-form, and he was sure that Professor Büren, the witness whom he regarded as an expert, would have to face considerable refutation when – as was inevitable – this case came before the Appeal Court. As for him, *he* could take neither the alleged underlying contradiction between art and society nor the alleged provocation into consideration in his pleadings. For him art implied something too subjective, too fortuitous. Such a decision must be made at 'other and higher levels'. He requested – and he was still smiling at the place where a crucifix had once hung – he requested, in his capacity as representative of the state whose very foundations, so to speak, had been assaulted by this offence – he requested two years' imprisonment for Johann Heinrich Georg Gruhl, two and a half years for Georg Gruhl, full restitution of all damage, and *no* allowance for remand custody, which had in any event been a transparent farce. Still smiling, he sat down, turning now toward the two accused; they showed no emotion, whereas Bergnolte, seated behind them, had given a perceptible start as Kugl-Egger announced his demands.

Stollfuss, who listened to the demands with a smile, now asked Hermes with customary courtesy to state his case, 'but without, I am sure you will understand, Herr Hermes, going into too much detail.'

Hermes, whose pleadings were subsequently described by all the lawyers present, and especially by Bergnolte, as 'magnificently fair' and brief, rose smilingly to his feet. He looked round the room, eyes pausing to take in the expression on the face of his aunt Agnes Hall – later described by Schroer as 'tranquil, lit from within' – and then said that he too was aware of the unique character of the case, and of the subjects under discussion; it was precisely for this reason that he re-gretted the 'clever manipulation within the press' which had prevented the public from learning much, if anything, about the events now being dealt with in this court. Be that as it may, he wished to be brief : his clients had confessed to the offence, they had done nothing whatever to impede the hearing of the evidence, and they had admitted to 'having gone somewhat too far'; not only were they prepared to make good the damage they had caused – restitution *had already* been made, thanks to the generosity of 'one of our fellow citizens, a well-known and be-loved figure in our community', who had presented him with a blank cheque. To him, as attorney for the defence, the whole affair was so clear it almost hurt – personally, he loved compli-cated cases; this one was so straightforward that it was almost a reflection on his professional honour. Dr Grähn, the economist, had described the modern economic process as relentless and remorseless; in other words, this fact had been confirmed by an expert and applied directly to Gruhl senior's financial situation. Had it by any chance (and here Hermes looked with *sincere* affability at his colleague Kugl-Egger and with *respectful* affa-bility at Dr Stollfuss) had it by any chance occurred to them that the work of art created by the two accused men – and confirmed as such by a professor – might have been intended to express that very relentlessness and remorselessness? He was well aware that the interpretation of works of art was a hit-or-miss affair, but he was willing to risk this interpretation. Incidentally, the remorselessness of the new art trend known as a 'Happening' had been publicly acknowledged in a highly respected national daily to which no breath of suspicion attached; in fact, there had even been a discussion in the Federal Parliament concerning the role of the Bundeswehr in a similar event. However, he did not wish to avoid the issue and ignore the two charges: public mischief and property damage. But was it not possible that, by its very nature, all art, *every* example of artistic expression, contained these two elements, because all art, since it changed, transformed, and sometimes even destroyed material, entailed property damage in terms of any theory inimical to art? He was aware, Hermes said, indicating by a glance at Stollfuss that he was approaching the end, he was well aware that the state could not automatically accept all this; but might not to-day's proceedings at least contribute in some small measure toward clarifying the relationship of the state, of the public, to art – in which the elements of both charges had been shown to inhere – by leading to the acquittal of both the accused? Yes, he was requesting acquittal, and also that the costs of the proceedings be borne by the public treasury. There was one more point he must mention, added Hermes, who had already sat down but now got up again: regarding the Bundeswehr's claims for restitution a question arose which he begged the court to decide. In accepting restitution, was the Bundeswehr not under an obligation to surrender the instrument of the work of art, the wreck of the jeep; surely his clients had a claim to that instrument once they had made good the loss and he reserved the right to pursue this aspect of the matter.

During the brief recess (called, purely as a formality, by Stollfuss because he deemed it wise to preserve the dignity of the court and its conventions by interposing at least a symbolic interval before he pronounced judgement), during the brief re-

153

cess everyone except Bergnolte remained in the courtroom; the two Gruhls whispered freely with Fräulein Hall, and Hermes with Kugl-Egger, who told Hermes with a smile that Frau Schroer really was a 'fantastic creature'. He could now taste that she had spiked the water not only with brandy but with sedative drops – disguised, 'concealed', as it were, by the brandy : he was going to think over the whole affair in peace and quiet for a few days, and decide whether he shouldn't protest and revoke the 'tactics advised', as Hermes no doubt knew, 'by a higher level'; only Aussem did not leave his seat, being busy with his records, to which, as he later confessed, he was giving a certain literary polish. Bergnolte, intending to catch the last train, which left Birglar at 12.30 a.m. for the city, went out for a few minutes to settle his account with Frau Schroer. To his surprise he found Frau Hermes and Frau Kugl-Egger in her kitchen; the former, who was sipping a cup of bouillon with obvious relish, laid a finger to her lips; the latter, anxious but at the same time already reassured, was listening to Frau Schroer's account of her husband's attack and its treatment, and to Frau Schroer's opinion that 'this Gruhl business' would be 'an ordeal for any district attorney who had been told to pull his punches'. Bergnolte's sudden appearance was greeted with no particular enthusiasm by any of the three ladies : Frau Hermes not only laid her finger to her lips but frowned and asked Frau Schroer, not very softly, whether she had 'heard a knock at the door'; Frau Schroer said she had not. Frau Kugl-Egger (who had had an argument with the decorator because he had tried to insist on a certain colour scheme derived a little too smugly from a night-school course in colour-harmony), Frau Kugl-Egger had of course been informed by Frau Hermes, her own husband, and Herr Hermes that Bergnolte was here to spy, and let slip an 'Oh heavens!' such as might have escaped her at the sudden appearance of a disagreeable animal. Finally Frau Schroer, who knew perfectly well what Bergnolte's rank and function were, contented herself with a rather brusque 'Yes?' to which Bergnolte who, as he said later, was 'not going to be put off by these women', replied by asking the cost of 'his recent meal'. Frau

Schroer had been told by Sterck, the sheriff's officer, that 'there was a chance this man might become' Stollfuss's successor, so she took the opportunity of 'making it clear right from the start, who was in charge here' and told him, none too pleasantly, that seventy pfennigs would cover it. This, 'like almost everything else in Birglar', seemed 'suspicious' to Bergnolte; incapable of correctly interpreting Frau Schroer's pert manner, not realizing that she was far from innocent of a certain erotic explosiveness – suspecting 'an attempt, although a minimal one, at bribery', and unaware that the best way of responding to such courtesy-hospitality is not to offer money but to bring a box of chocolates or, even belatedly, send flowers – he insisted, somewhat shortly, 'on paying the full and proper price for the meal'. Frau Schroer – her eyes on the other two women (who could hardly contain themselves), posing a little and quite aware that she was posing – calculated for Bergnolte's benefit that twenty-five pfennigs was plenty for a boiled egg; she would consider the bouillon, which she was accustomed to preparing in large quantities, also covered by twenty-five pfennigs, and, on second thoughts, she felt twenty pfennigs was rather excessive for a slice of bread and butter; she therefore 'requested the counsellor' to settle for sixty pfennigs: she would like to make it clear that she was not operating a tavern but a 'courtesy snack room'. While she was calculating, first submissively, then with an edge to her sub-missiveness, and finally with bitter submissiveness, she let her eyes – her expression varying with each person present – glide from Frau Hermes to Frau Kugl-Egger, from there to Berg-nolte, and then all the way round to Bergnolte again. The latter – 'wavering', as he later put it, 'between capitulation and revolt' – opted for capitulation; at the last moment it crossed his mind that a tip, which, incredibly enough, he had still been consider-ing at this stage of the negotiations, would 'go down very badly indeed'. Looking, as Frau Schroer described it afterward to the two Gruhls and her husband, 'thoroughly pissed', he counted out the coins from his purse on to the kitchen table and, as he later admitted, was 'thankful to have the right change'; leaving the kitchen in a chastened mood and forgetting in his discomfiture

155

to say good-bye to his colleagues' wives, he stopped to listen at the door, convinced that there would be a burst of feminine laughter behind him. He waited and listened in vain; when he heard the sound of feet scraping and chairs being moved in the courtroom he went in quickly, unaware that at precisely that moment Frau Hermes, who after his exit had laid her finger to her lips again, 'released' her own laughter and that of the other two women.

Aussem confessed that, a few days later, while dictating his stenographic record of the judge's summing-up to Stollfuss's secretary, he had again felt his eyes moisten; 'not tears exactly, but, well, you know what I mean'. By the time Stollfuss re-entered the courtroom it was almost midnight; and Bergnolte, who arrived just in time, described himself later to his wife as an 'insufferable, incorrigible pedant' because he found himself continually looking at the time and 'thinking about that damn last train'. At the back of his mind was a 'persistent anxiety about the considerable cab fare I might have to claim from the government – there's no getting away from it, you know; I'm a bureaucrat at heart, and always will be, and what's more, I'm proud of it'. Finally even Bergnolte forgot the time, while Agnes claimed that, from Stollfuss's very first words, she was absolutely lost to the world. Stollfuss first spoke without his biretta; he looked at Agnes, the Gruhls, Hermes, Aussem, Kugl-Egger, and Agnes again, this time frankly and incontestably nodding to her; then he smiled because Frau Hermes and Frau Kugl-Egger came in, quietly, like people arriving late for church and not wanting to interrupt the service. As long as he spoke without his biretta Stollfuss touched only on personal matters; he would, he said, soon be taking off his robe; this trial, so he had been told, was not only probably but certainly his last – his last public appearance. He regretted that those citizens of Birglar County whom he had been obliged to judge and sentence were not all assembled here; they represented an imposing number, 'a fair-sized throng'; not all, but most of them had really been quite nice people, a bit mixed up, a bad streak showing

156

now and again, but on the whole – and he included Hepperle, convicted on a morals charge – 'really nice'. But this trial – and he regarded this as a special favour – was the nicest of all: the accused, all the witnesses, yes *all* – an allusion, in Agnes Hall's opinion, to Sanni Seiffert – the district attorney, the defence attorney, the public, and especially the distinguished lady over there among the spectators who had attended literally all his public trials. He was sorry about the incident with Herr Kirffel, the tax inspector, and admitted that he was to blame; he would apologize again to Kirffel. The complicated nature of the case – here he must unfortunately differ from his colleague, Herr Hermes – had made him forget himself. As for the case itself – and he still did not put on his biretta – well, he realized that his judgement could not be a final one; this case transcended not only his competence as a county court judge but the competence of even the highest courts in the land; it involved 'the crux, the very cross-roads, of human life', and he was far from being the man to pronounce a valid judgement on such a case as that. A judgement he would give, and for *him* it was a final judgement, but would it satisfy other and higher levels? He didn't know, and he was almost tempted to say he *hoped* not; for the objective which, as a judge, he had always striven toward but probably seldom achieved – justice – was something he had fallen further short of in this trial than in any trial he had ever conducted: he had done *justice* to the deed, the event, the operation, the perpetration – would Herr Aussem kindly refrain from putting any of these words in quotation marks? – but he could not do *justice* to 'the matter as a whole'. He had been convinced – and now he put on his biretta – by both the defence and the prosecution; but he personally considered that, while 'public mischief' had been proven, 'property damage' had not. Yet he had also been convinced by the accused. They had frankly stated something which he as a judge had to admit: that in a matter of this kind there was no such thing as justice, nor did they, the accused, expect it. That he, a judge, should declare himself helpless in this instance, that as his last case he should have been given one which so clearly exemplified the inadequacy

157

of human laws: *this* was for him the most beautiful farewell gift from that blindfolded goddess who had shown him so many faces: sometimes that of a whore, now and again that of a woman in trouble, never that of a saint, but more often than not that of a groaning, tormented creature expressing itself through his, the judge's agency; a creature part animal, part human, and part – a very little part – goddess. He was sentencing the accused to full restitution of damage and ordering the Bundeswehr to surrender the art-instrument, for it was not Professor Büren's testimony alone that had convinced him of the accuracy of this description. However, if this trend of 'creating works of art, or moments fraught with art' were to spread, the consequences could be disastrous, especially since, like everything that becomes popularized, it would probably degenerate into the trite, the artsy-craftsy. He was therefore obliged – and he was doing so without compunction or scruple – to sentence the accused to six weeks' imprisonment, a term which had already been served by the remand custody. He felt sure the accused would not take it amiss if he gave them some advice – and he took off his biretta again – seeing that he was old enough to be their father and grandfather respectively: they ought to make themselves independent of the state by not offering the state any opportunity – he was referring here to Gruhl senior's tax arrears – to restrict them in their liberty; and, in paying this tribute, it was up to them to be as cunning as foxes, for the relentlessness and remorselessness of the economic process had been definitely *proved* in this court by an expert who was regarded as a competent authority, and it was a mistake to face a relentless, remorseless society unarmed. It was twenty-five minutes past midnight – subsequently, at Stollfuss's request, altered in the records at 11:46 p.m., because he did not wish to see the new day 'encumbered with this affair' – when Stollfuss, resuming his official tone of voice, ordered the accused to step forward and state whether they accepted the sentence. The two men conferred very briefly, scarcely uttering a word and looking for guidance at Hermes, who nodded; with their attorney they stepped forward and stated that they would accept the sentence.

Stollfuss left the courtroom very quickly. He personally felt not only much less emotion than might have been expected, he felt none at all as he hung his robe on the hook in the dimly lit corridor. He passed his hands over his bald head, rubbed his tired eyes, and, as he bent forward to take his hat from the peg, he looked down and saw Bergnolte running across the dark playground, and smiled.

Five

Down in the courtroom fatigue and emotion maintained a balance: for some minutes one would hold the other in check, until fatigue got the upper hand, tears of emotion remained unshed, and sighs gave way to yawns. Even the Gruhls were exhausted, conscious at last of how much momentum had been concealed in proceedings which to them had seemed a long-drawn-out repetition of the same old statements. If Frau Schroer's term, a 'marathon', had seemed inappropriate throughout the day, they now realized how quickly it all happened. Now, too, the brief weeks of custody suddenly appeared infinitely long, and the sudden access of liberty struck them – as Gruhl senior put it – 'like a hammer blow'. They had no desire to return that night to their cold, neglected home in Huskirchen; and yet to ask Frau Schmitz to put them up at the Duhr Terraces seemed inadvisable in view of the lateness of the hour and Herr Schmitz's declaration of hostilities as conveyed by the quality of the supper. Their request to be taken back to their cells was firmly turned down by Schroer, who maintained that 'it was government accommodation, after all, and, damn it, Hännchen, we aren't a hotel, you know'; besides, he went on, Gruhl must realize that it wasn't a good idea to risk drawing public attention to the Elysian conditions in the Birglar jail; what was more, he, Schroer, didn't feel inclined to turn himself into 'a buffoon of the law courts'. Since Stollfuss had already left and it didn't seem right to telephone him; since Kugl-Egger declared he was too exhausted to make any decision at all, let alone such a delicate one – all he wanted was a couple of pints of beer and forty-eight hours' sleep; and since Hermes said it would be unwise to seek the hospitality of the law after such a verdict, the Gruhls accepted Agnes Hall's offer, tendered with much diffidence, to spend the night at her house. They were enticed by the prospect of oxtail soup, asparagus ('canned, unfortunately'), and chicken salad, for which she had a special recipe; she was sorry she had no beer, but she could offer them a bottle of good wine; and besides, perhaps it was 'not too soon to start discussing' the next Happening, in which she was prepared to participate musically. She had read that old pianos were much sought after for these occasions, and mightn't one take a *new* automobile and an *old* piano – she had two in her basement. ... But here she was tactfully cut short by Hermes, who found the discussion of such plans 'in the presence of the district attorney rather too macabre': he laid a hand on his aunt's shoulder and steered her politely out of the court-house, followed by the Gruhls. Lisa Schroer, who was now – it was about one in the morning – 'coming to the end of her tether' as she said later, announced the arrival of the taxi for the Kugl-Eggers, who left the court-house together with Herr and Frau Hermes; only Aussem stayed behind, busy, in what Frau Schroer called his 'piddly handwriting', completing his records.

The only person who might have been described as still fresh was Frau Hermes. She had spent a pleasant afternoon having coffee with her friend, with whom she had discussed a topic that would have justified her reputation of being dedicated to 'The Pill'; then she had slept for a couple of hours, and finally gone for a stroll past 'Küpper's Tree' to Huskirchen, where she arrived at the Kugl-Eggers' apartment just in time to lend her support to Marlies in the latter's battle with the decorator, considered by both women to be the product of misguided and excessive education. Moreover, she had been triumphant, due to her ability to understand the comments muttered by the decorator in the heavy dialect of this sugar-beet region, to grasp their considerable coarseness, and to pay him back in his own coin – as to both coarseness and dialect. Hermes, tired and pale, and appearing to have aged by several years, leaned on his wife's arm as he almost staggered home through silent, sleeping Birglar; he protested vehemently when his wife, 'drawn like a moth to the flame', wanted to turn aside toward the only window in Birglar still showing a light, the printing office of the *Duhr Valley Courier*, saying she wanted to go in and 'give them a piece of her mind'. Although there was little enough resistance left in him, Hermes managed to awaken the pity of his determined wife, for whom it was evidently no small sacrifice to have to renounce a nocturnal confrontation with Hollweg.

Bergnolte had already reached the first suburban station of the city before Frau Schroer could finally close the door after Aussem and sit down with her husband for a bite to eat; without hesitation or scruple she served the margarine and liver-sausage sandwiches left behind by the Gruhls, because she was 'too tired even to pick up a knife'. Acting on instructions – 'even if it takes till three in the morning!' Grellber had said – Bergnolte hastened to the nearest taxi stand and was driven out to the quiet suburb where he was relieved to see lights still burning in Grellber's villa; throughout the evening he had been tormented by the idea that he might be compelled to get the president out of bed by a prolonged ringing of the doorbell – something which, orders or no orders, would have gone very much against the grain. However, not only did Grellber have the lights on, he seemed to have been waiting for the sound of the approaching taxi; by the time Bergnolte had paid off the driver (who morosely muttered something about 'at one in the morning the tips are usually a bit higher' and complied with Bergnolte's request for a receipt, with obvious reluctance, by ripping the sheet off the pad, as Bergnolte reported later, with 'the most maddening insolence'), by the time Bergnolte had overcome all these unavoidable delays Grellber had not only appeared at the front door and opened it but had already come down the steps to meet Bergnolte, placed a fatherly hand on his shoulder, and asked as they entered the house: 'Well, wasn't the food first-rate? You can still find cooks in these out-of-the-way little places, eh?' Despite his experience to the contrary and the contemptible betrayal of his palate, Bergnolte replied: 'Yes, first-rate, I'd almost be inclined to say: unique!' In his study,

162

where fresh cigar smoke provided a contemporary masculinity and stale cigar smoke a traditional one, where, as Bergnolte later described it, an enormous old standard lamp with a green silk shade dispensed a 'subdued dignity' and crowded bookshelves betokened a sound professional background, Grellber, whose generous nature was not only manifest in his expression but could have been confirmed by almost all his students and subordinates ('except for a few bad eggs') – Grellber, 'as an exception, permitted cigarettes in this sacred domain' but did not ask Bergnolte to take off his coat. Grellber laughed at the story of the district attorney's nervous collapse and at the sentence he had demanded, smiled when he heard of Stollfuss's verdict, and made a note of the names: Kolb, Büren, and Kuttke. Even the way in which he occasionally interrupted Bergnolte's report whenever the latter, instead of giving a brief sketch of the persons mentioned, threatened to digress into legal or philosophical speculations – even that was as courteous and gracious as the terminating gesture with which he declared the conversation to be at an end; 'without the least fuss', in the manner familiar to Bergnolte, he picked up the telephone himself, dialled, and personally ordered a taxi for his guest, whom he wished a 'good night's rest, you've certainly earned it'. Bergnolte found it especially tactful of Grellber to have refrained on *this* particular day from mentioning the county court appointment that not only had been promised Bergnolte but to which he was entitled.

Knowing he would wake no one but would only be speaking into an automatic tape recorder, Grellber – after watching Bergnolte drive off in the taxi – dialled the number of the member of the legislature who had been with him when he had met Hollweg the previous evening after the theatre. He dictated verdict and sentence into the tape recorder, along with the names Kuttke, Major Troeger, and Colonel von Greblothe; then followed with a few well-chosen sentences in which he requested the member of the legislature to ask the provincial Minister of Education – who, although not a fellow party member, was a personal friend of the member of the legislature – for a full report on a certain Professor Büren. He replaced the receiver, and debated for a few minutes whether it was feasible and sufficiently important at this hour to telephone a certain dignitary of the Church with whom he was on close enough terms to warrant rousing him in the middle of the night, if the circumstances justified it. Then, the receiver already in his hand, he recalled that, according to Bergnolte's report, only *two* outside spectators had been present during Father Kolb's testimony, and he postponed his call to the next morning. (When he did finally call the prelate at eleven the next morning, the first thing the latter asked was *how many* spectators had been present. When Grellber named the figure two the prelate burst out laughing, so heartily – for his age too heartily – that he choked and couldn't get his breath back; he had to cut short the conversation before he could tell Grellber that Kolb customarily delivered himself of his 'strange views' on Sundays, in the presence of some two or three hundred members of his flock.)

Aussem was the last to leave the court-house. Frau Schroer – who liked him, was related to him through his mother, and insisted on calling her Auntie when he was 'off duty' – invited him to help them eat up Schmitz's liver-sausage sandwiches, but he declined and strolled across the former playground toward the Duhr bridge. Having overcome his weariness with cold water, Aussem found himself in a mood of euphoria mingled with tenderness for the old judge; he yearned for human company and, imagining where this was most readily to be found, turned off to the right beyond the St Nepomuk statue toward Agnes Hall's villa. He was surprised to find it in total darkness, but in the doorway, to his somewhat lesser surprise, he found young Gruhl and Eva Schmitz in an embrace which he later described as 'almost statuesque'; he quickly changed direction, his happy mood waning: not only was jealousy gnawing at him, he was also depressed at having to by-pass Sanni Seiffert's place. She had threatened, if he didn't pay his debts, to tell his father, Aussem the shoemaker, 'what a big show-off he was, buying champagne all round'; and he felt that, in this almost lyrical mood, he lacked the will power to persuade the glib Sanni to extend his credit. He was 'about to resign himself to the fact', or at any rate submit to his fate, that he would have to go home, where the smell of leather bothered him – 'not always, mind you, but sometimes' – more than the brooding melancholy of his father who had been bereaved of his young wife so many years ago. At that moment he suddenly saw – 'and I realized for the first time the hope and joy that those words "a light in darkness" can express' – a light in the printing office of the *Duhr Valley Courier*; he hurried toward it, found the door open, entered, and broke in on the violent dispute going on between his political friend Hollweg and Brehsel, who was 'close to' the same party; as he did so it struck him for the first time, as he said later on, 'how extraordinarily fatuous Hollweg's nice handsome face can seem all of a sudden'. His tie pulled down, his shirtsleeves rolled up, 'brandishing a bottle of beer like a bricklayer', Hollweg was once more seated at the Linotype machine (incidentally, the *Duhr Valley Courier* compositor referred to these efforts as being absolutely 'without rhyme or reason' since he, the compositor, usually had to reset the whole mess anyway; yet he couldn't expect to get paid for the extra hours because of course nobody knew – and Hollweg was the last person who must be allowed to find out – that this 'fooling around in the middle of the night was just so much waste of time'). He was in the midst of an argument with Brehsel, who was obviously annoyed, over the word 'protruding' which he had failed to find in the description of Schewen's face; in two national dailies and one national weekly, Hollweg said, he had read the adjective 'protruding' as applied by three different reporters to the lips of Schewen, the child murderer, so why had Brehsel omitted to use it? For the simple reason, said Brehsel, who by this time was past concealing either his impatience or his contempt for Hollweg's fatuousness, that Schewen's lips *weren't* protruding; they weren't even 'thick', they simply had 'no special characteristics at all'; he would call them 'normal lips', except that the expression 'normal lips' struck him as being rather ludicrous. Did he imagine then, asked Hollweg (now – despite his 'working-man's pose', which struck Aussem as 'pretty phoney' – suddenly the boss again), did he imagine that all the reporters, the whole lot of them, were blind, stupid, or prejudiced, and that he, Herr Wolfgang Brehsel, 'was the only one with eyes in his head and a monopoly on the truth about Schewen's lips?' No, said Brehsel, he wasn't the only one with eyes in his head, and he had no monopoly on the truth; in fact the truth could not be monopolized, but the fact remained that Schewen's lips were not protruding, at least they hadn't been all that day – and he had been watching Schewen for eight hours on end – they certainly hadn't been on that particular day! Aha, Hollweg said, now one of the boys again and inviting Aussem to help himself to a beer from the case, Brehsel was already retreating to *hadn't been*. A photo from the archives, showing Schewen unshaven, a cigarette between his lips, was rejected by Brehsel as evidence of the protrusion of the lips; he put a cigarette in his own mouth in such a way that it pointed upward, demonstrating how his own lips, which were not in the least protruding, did in fact, when pursed to grip the cigarette, show a 'certain protrusion'. He pointed out that it was on the basis of this photo, the only one to have been published since the trial began, that the reporters of the other newspapers had used the term 'protruding'; as for him, he refused to allow the term 'protruding' to be inserted in his report; besides, the trial of Schewen was 'remarkably dull', and he suggested that, starting tomorrow, no, today – it was already one-thirty and he was dog-tired – they use the news agency reports, 'the ones with the protruding lips, for all I care, but *I'm* not going to write that he has protruding lips'. Aussem, who had never really noticed before how fatuous Hollweg was, and who was secretly hoping that Hollweg would invite him to Sanni Seiffert's place, which stayed open till four a.m., was called upon to act as arbitrator; he was aware of a fleeting temptation to decide in favour of Hollweg, thus ensuring himself, as he knew from experience, of two free whiskies-and-soda. Later, on reviewing the occurrence and, with his desire for accuracy, trying to pinpoint whether the determining factor had not been the prospect – which suddenly seemed 'incredibly boring and tedious' – of spending the rest of the night in Hollweg's company, he decided to justify his verdict in favour of Brehsel as having been factual rather than emotional. He had based his argument on his considerable experience with the reports of eye-witnesses, 'even highly intelligent ones', who were usually guided by prejudice rather than judgement or their senses; actually, Aussem went on, the only really reliable, accurate eye-witness he knew was old Inspector Kirffel, who would certainly not hesitate to describe Schewen's lips as *not protruding* if they didn't seem protruding to him, no matter if he had read in half a dozen newspapers, local or national, that they *were* protruding. In every way, he said, Kirffel was – but here Hollweg interrupted him with the same asperity which had offended Aussem that noon at the Duhr Terraces, saying he was fed to the teeth with 'rooting around in this stuffy Birglar provincialism'; *he* had work to do. Very well then, he wouldn't insist on the word 'protruding' because he respected *freedom*, even when it ran counter to his convictions; but as for the names Kirffel, Hall, Kirffel, and yet again Hall, he could hardly bear to hear them any more. When Aussem asked him whether he could still bear to hear the name Gruhl, Hollweg became positively aggressive, a thing he rarely did, and said *he*, Hollweg, wasn't a bureaucrat; his salary wasn't deposited regularly in the bank the first of every month; *he* had work to do. Brehsel hastily said good-bye, leaving it to Aussem to remain behind for a few minutes and listen to Hollweg 'harp away' on his favourite themes: that it was vital to freedom and democracy to keep newspapers like the *Duhr Valley Courier* free and independent, and that to sit down at the Linotype machine and operate it himself was neither a hobby nor a pastime. Aussem, prompted less by politeness than by the fatigue that welled up in him again after the beer he had just finished, stayed behind for a few minutes listening to Hollweg's unexpected diatribe; then he said good night and went home. The familiar smell of leather had long ceased to haunt him, he almost craved it.

More about Penguins and Pelicans

Penguinews, which appears every month, contains details of all the new books issued by Penguins as they are published. From time to time it is supplemented by the *Penguin Stock List* which includes around 5,000 titles.

A specimen copy of *Penguinews* will be sent to you free on request. Please write to Dept EP, Penguin Books Ltd, Harmondsworth, Middlesex, for your copy.

In the U.S.A.: For a complete list of books available from Penguins in the United States write to Dept CS, Penguin Books, 625 Madison Avenue, New York, New York 10022.

In Canada: For a complete list of books available from Penguins in Canada write to Penguin Books Canada Ltd, 2801 John Street, Markham, Ontario L3R 1B4.

Thomas Mann

The Magic Mountain

Written by the most important figure in German literature in the first half of this century, *The Magic Mountain* is in Mann's own words 'a dialectic novel'. The setting (like that of his earlier *Tristan*) is a sanatorium high in the Swiss Alps; and it is into this rarefied and extra-mundane atmosphere, devoted to and organized in the service of ill-health, that young Hans Castorp comes, intending at first to stay for three weeks but remaining seven years. With him are a cosmopolitan collection of people: an Italian liberal, a Jew turned Jesuit, a doctor, a seductive Russian woman, and his cousin Joachim who desperately longs for action and returns to the 'lower realities' of the world, only coming back to the sanatorium to die. Their occupation is discussion, and in this they indulge relentlessly and with an Olympian arrogance and detachment from the outer world.

But love, war, and emotions all effect and influence their conversation and they are indeed a microcosm and symbol of the pre-First-World-War society below them – of a sick Europe.

The Magic Mountain won the Nobel Prize for Literature in 1929.

Also published in Penguins

Buddenbrooks
Death in Venice
Death in Venice/Tristan/Tonio Kröger
Doctor Faustus
The Holy Sinner
Little Herr Friedemann and Other Stories
Lotte in Weimar

Günter Grass

The Tin Drum

Certainly the strangest, probably the greatest novel to come out of Germany in years.

The best-seller that scandalized Germany, impressed France, and sold by the hundred thousand in Britain and the U.S.A.

'Maleficent masterpiece' – *Daily Telegraph*

'An off-beat masterpiece' – *Listener*

'The nearest thing to a literary masterpiece his generation is capable of producing' – *Spectator*

Also published in Penguins

Dog Years
Cat and Mouse
From the Diary of a Snail
Local Anaesthetic

Hermann Hesse

Steppenwolf

Hermann Hesse's poetical novel, *Steppenwolf*, was written some twenty years before he won the Nobel Prize for Literature in 1946. This Faust-like and magical story of the humanization of a middle-aged misanthrope was described in the *New York Times* as 'a savage indictment of bourgeois society'. But, as the author notes in this edition, *Steppenwolf* is a book which has been violently misunderstood. This self-portrait of a man who felt himself to be half-human and half-wolf can also be seen as a plea for rigorous self-examination and an indictment of intellectual hypocrisy.

The Glass Bead Game

The Glass Bead Game is an ultra-aesthetic game which is played by the scholars, creamed off in childhood and nurtured in élite schools, in the kingdom of Castalia.

The Master of the Glass Bead Game, Joseph Knecht, holds the most exalted office in Castalia. He personifies the detachment, serenity, and aesthetic vision which rewards a life dedicated to perfection of the intellect.

But can, indeed, should man live isolated from hunger, family, children, women, in a perfect world where passions are tamed by meditation, where academic discipline and order are paramount?

This is Hermann Hesse's great novel. It is a major contribution to contemporary philosophic literature and has a powerful vision of universality, the inner unity of man's cultural ideals, and his search for personal perfection and social responsibility.

Also published in Penguins

Narziss and Goldmund
Peter Camazind
Gertrude
The Prodigy

Also by Arthur Koestler

Darkness at Noon

'One of the few books written in this epoch which will survive it. It is written from terrible experience, from knowledge of the men whose struggles of mind and body he describes. Apart from its sociological importance, it is written with a subtlety and an economy which class it as great literature. I have read it twice without feeling that I have learned more than half of what it has to offer me.

'Mr Koestler approaches the problem of ends and means, of love and truth and social organization, through the thoughts of an Old Bolshevik, Rubashov, as he awaits death in a G.P.U. prison' – Kingsley Martin in the *New Statesman*

'A brilliant book full of indignant bewilderment, of resentment against chaos, of pity for all that is pitiable' – Robert Lynd in the *News Chronicle*

'A remarkable book, a grimly fascinating interpretation of the logic of the Russian Revolution, indeed of all revolutionary dictatorships, and at the same time a tense and subtly intellectualized drama of prison psychology' – *The Times Literary Supplement*

Also published in Penguins

Arrival and Departure

Franz Kafka

The Trial

The Trial was the first of Kafka's books to appear as a
Penguin. The work of this strange and mystifying Czech
writer, who died of consumption in 1924, has earned him a
unique reputation in modern European literature and has
provoked many endeavours to 'interpret' his view of life. *The
Trial* relates the perplexing experiences of a man ostensibly
arrested on a charge which is never specified, but within the
pattern of the complicated narrative Kafka is trying to
elucidate some of the fundamental dilemmas of human life.
The story is a Pilgrim's Progress of the sub-conscious, the
phantasmagoria of a sensitive mind oppressed and
bewildered by the burden of living. It reads like the transcript
of a protracted, implacable dream in which reality is
entangled with imagination.

Also published in Penguins

The Castle
Metamorphosis and other stories
America

Heinrich Böll in Penguins

Group Portrait With Lady

'Leni [the central character] is seen through a series of interviews with witnesses who make up this huge "group portrait". This works brilliantly as a parody of fashionable documentary; then by making the story resonant with overlapping echoes; and finally by counterpointing these voices of the imagination with the terrible dead language of real documents of Nazi bureaucracy' – *Guardian*

Children Are Civilians Too

A collection of the most representative of Böll's short stories, written between 1947 and 1951. In them the author concentrates on ordinary men and women as they struggled with hunger, fear and pain in the aftermath of the war.

To be published

And Where Were You, Adam?
The Train Was on Time